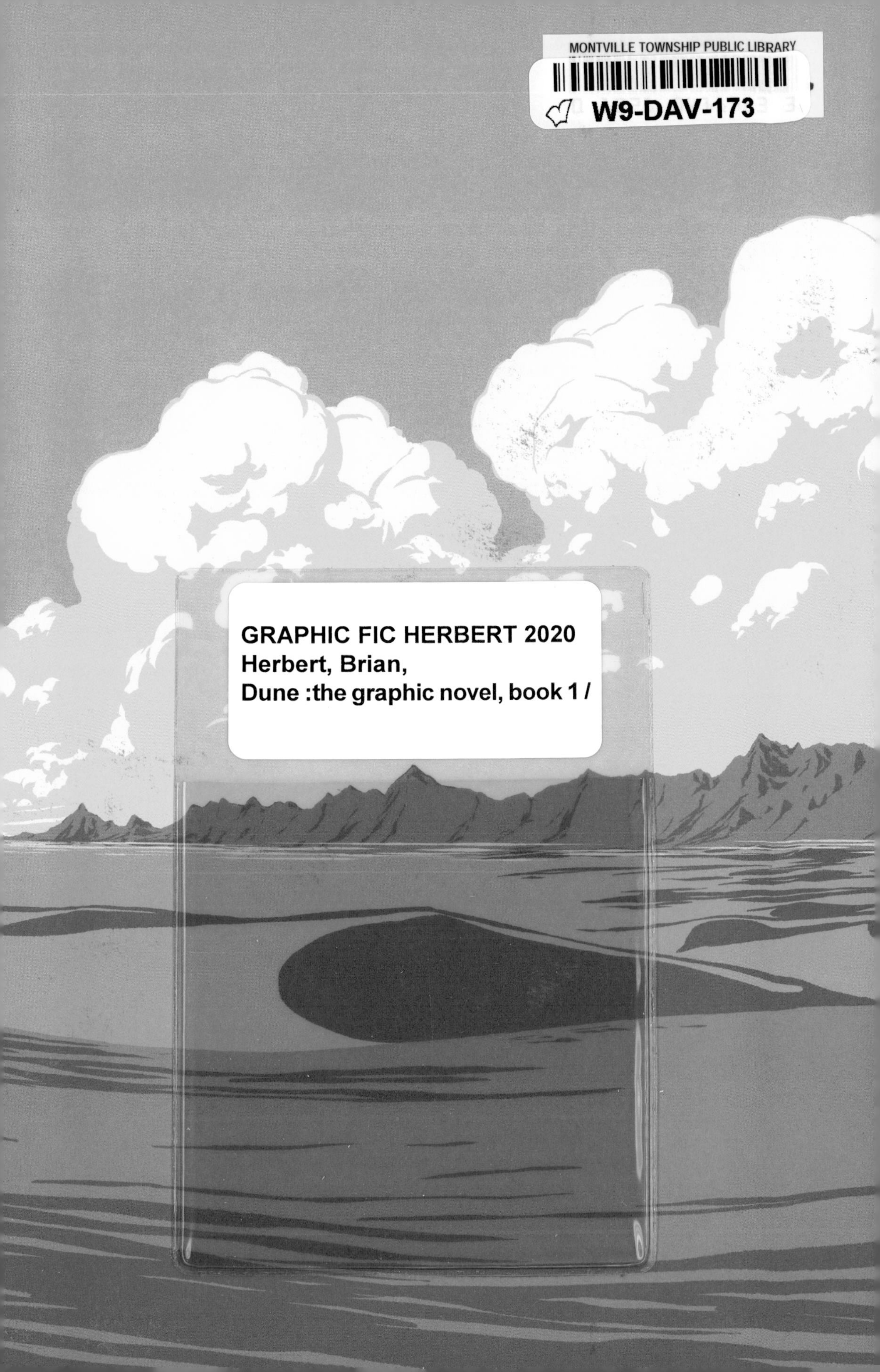

FRANK HERBERT'S

DUNE

THE GRAPHIC NOVEL, BOOK 1

ABRAMS COMICARTS
NEW YORK

FRANK HERBERT'S
DUNE

THE GRAPHIC NOVEL, BOOK 1

ADAPTED BY

BRIAN HERBERT AND **KEVIN J. ANDERSON**

ILLUSTRATED BY **RAÚL ALLÉN** AND **PATRICIA MARTÍN**

For **FRANK HERBERT**,
who read the early drafts of *Dune* to his
family, and to his loving wife of nearly
four decades, **BEVERLY HERBERT**, who
always provided wise counsel

Project Manager: Charles Kochman
Editor: Charlotte Greenbaum
Designers: Megan Kelchner and Charice Silverman
Managing Editor: Lisa Silverman
Production Manager: Erin Vandeveer

Art assistants: Jesús R. Pastrana (pencil and inks),
Guillermo Ortego (inks), David Astruga (designs and color), Alex J. Brady (designs)
Additional colors: Mónica Jaspe Garfia
Endpapers: Jesús R. Pastrana and Raúl Allén

Cataloging-in-Publication Data has been applied for and may be obtained from the
Library of Congress.

ISBN 978-1-4197-3150-1
eISBN 978-1-64700-182-7

Printed and bound in USA
10 9 8 7 6 5 4 3 2 1

Abrams ComicArts books are available at special discounts when purchased in quantity
for premiums and promotions as well as fundraising or educational use. Special editions
can also be created to specification. For details, contact specialsales@abramsbooks.com
or the address below.

Abrams ComicArts® is a registered trademark of Harry N. Abrams, Inc.

ABRAMS The Art of Books
195 Broadway, New York, NY 10007
abramsbooks.com

ACKNOWLEDGMENTS

From Brian Herbert and Kevin J. Anderson: We'd like to acknowledge the hard work, attention to detail, and patience of Charles Kochman and Charlotte Greenbaum of Abrams ComicArts; Bill Sienkiewicz, Raúl Allén, and Patricia Martín for their artistic contributions; Byron Merritt and Kim Herbert of Herbert Properties LLC; as well as our literary agents, John Silbersack and Mary Alice Kier; our attorney, Marcy Morris; and our incredible wives, Jan Herbert and Rebecca Moesta.

From Raúl Allén and Patricia Martín: We want to thank everybody who made this book possible, particularly the team behind all these pages, for all their effort and passion. In particular Rebecca, Uge, Santi, Tesi, Miguel, and Samuel . . . Also, a big thank-you to our dear editor, Charlotte Greenbaum, and the Abrams team for their trust.

We also feel immensely grateful to our families for all the love and patience during these challenging days.

And to Raúl's brother, who shared his love of *Dune* and comics with Raúl. Wherever you are, this book is for you, Luis.

Special thanks to Borja Pindado, Aneke, Álvaro Cubero, Néstor Martínez, Antonio del Hoyo, Miguel Sastre, Adrián Rodríguez, Ruth Prado, Jesús R. Pastrana, and Sara Rodríguez; without their help, this book would not have been possible.

PREFACE

FRANK HERBERT'S CLASSIC *DUNE* IS A FANTASTIC VISUAL EXPERIENCE, an epic story that is the most beloved novel in science fiction. This monumental literary masterpiece, with larger-than-life characters, Machiavellian plot twists, and sweeping vistas of the desert and galaxy, is a perfect candidate to be adapted as a graphic novel. We are extremely pleased to present Frank Herbert's *DUNE: The Graphic Novel, Book 1: Dune.*

When we turned to the task of writing the script, we decided from the outset—with the full support of our publisher, Abrams—that this must be a definitive graphic novel treatment, a truly faithful adaptation of Frank Herbert's classic from 1965. We weren't interested in doing our interpretation of *Dune* or modifying the story to add our own special stamp. We wanted this to be pure *Dune*—chapter for chapter, scene for scene.

Naturally, this does not mean the inclusion of every gesture or line of dialogue—a picture is worth a thousand words, after all—but we wanted to convey the ambitious story the way Frank Herbert originally told it. Because the original novel is broken into three "books," the graphic novel will be released in three separate volumes.

Writing the script was only the first part of the challenge. Finding the right artists was critical. Working closely with the editorial team at Abrams ComicArts, we reviewed the work of various artists until we finally settled on the style and imagination of Bill Sienkiewicz for the cover and Raúl Allén and Patricia Martín for the interior. Then came the questions of character design, costumes, technology, settings, and the different planets beyond just Arrakis or Dune, the desert planet. In each case, we kept a watchful eye on the *Dune* canon that Frank Herbert laid out, and made certain that the art matched the vision he had for his incredible universe.

There have been previous cinematic adaptations of *Dune* . . . David Lynch's 1984 movie, the SciFi Channel miniseries, and the new Legendary movie, directed by Denis Villeneuve. While all these productions have their own aesthetic and visual language, we want this graphic novel to stand alone as a unique and independent work.

For the interior art of the graphic novel, working with Raúl Allén and Patricia Martín, as well as the editorial team at Abrams ComicArts, we have developed a general look and atmosphere for the pages and layouts. We are very excited about how this first volume turned out and look forward to the subsequent two books, which will complete our adaptation of the novel. We hope these Abrams publications bring a whole new audience to Frank Herbert's breathtaking universe of adventure, politics, religion, and ecology.

We first got together in 1997 to explore writing in the Dune universe, and since then we have written many international bestselling novels that expand on Dune's history and characters. In our novels, we have developed the full stories of Duke Leto, Lady Jessica, the Baron Harkonnen, the Padishah Emperor Shaddam IV, and his henchman Count Hasimir Fenring. We have traveled five thousand years further in the future to complete the epic that Frank Herbert outlined, and we have gone ten millennia deeper back in time to describe the origins of the Butlerian Jihad, the Fremen arriving on Arrakis, the establishment of the Bene Gesserit Sisterhood, the Mentats, the Navigators, and the Spacing Guild. We have written millions of words of original fiction—but this graphic novel is a special treat for us, to go to the heart of the source material, to bring Frank Herbert's original novel to life in exactly the way he envisioned it. In these illustrated pages, we want the legions of dedicated Dune fans to have an exciting new visual experience for the greatest science-fiction novel of all time.

Brian Herbert   *Kjfhl*

BRIAN HERBERT AND **KEVIN J. ANDERSON**

DEEP IN THE HUMAN UNCONSCIOUS
IS A PERVASIVE NEED FOR A
LOGICAL UNIVERSE THAT MAKES
SENSE. BUT THE REAL UNIVERSE IS
ALWAYS ONE STEP BEYOND LOGIC.

—FROM *COLLECTED SAYINGS OF MUAD'DIB* BY
THE PRINCESS IRULAN

ARRAKIS.

DUNE.

DESERT PLANET.

CALADAN.

A beginning is the time for taking the most delicate care that the balances are correct. This every sister of the Bene Gesserit knows.

To begin your study of the life of Muad'Dib, then, take care that you first place him in his time: born in the 57th year of the Padishah Emperor, Shaddam IV. And take the most special care that you locate Muad'Dib in his place: the planet Arrakis.

CASTLE CALADAN.

HOUSE ATREIDES IS IN THE FINAL FRENZY OF ACTIVITY TO PACK AND TRANSFER THEIR POSSESSIONS TO THE PLANET ARRAKIS—THE NEW FIEF OF DUKE LETO ATREIDES, GRANTED TO HIM BY EMPEROR SHADDAM IV.

AN OLD CRONE COMES TO VISIT THE MOTHER OF THE BOY PAUL.

REVEREND MOTHER MOHIAM. I...KNEW YOU WOULD COME. I AM READY.

IT IS TIME, JESSICA. I WOULD SEE YOUR SON.

HE'S ALREADY FIFTEEN.

YES, YOUR REVERENCE.

HE'S AWAKE AND LISTENING TO US. SLY LITTLE RASCAL. BUT ROYALTY HAS NEED OF SLYNESS. AND IF HE'S REALLY THE *KWISATZ HADERACH*, WELL...

SLEEP WELL, YOU SLY LITTLE RASCAL. TOMORROW YOU'LL NEED ALL YOUR FACULTIES TO MEET MY *GOM JABBAR*.

WHAT'S A GOM JABBAR? KWISATZ HADERACH?

AND WHY DID MY MOTHER CALL HER "YOUR REVERENCE"?

IS THIS SOMETHING I NEED TO KNOW BEFORE ARRAKIS?

NEXT MORNING...

PAUL? YOU'RE AWAKE. DID YOU SLEEP WELL?

YES, MOTHER. I WAS PRACTICING THE MIND-BODY LESSONS YOU TAUGHT ME.

STRIVING FOR THE FLOW-PERMANENCE WITHIN.

HURRY AND DRESS. REVEREND MOTHER IS WAITING.

WHO IS THE REVEREND MOTHER? I DREAMED OF HER ONCE.

SHE WAS MY TEACHER AT THE BENE GESSERIT SCHOOL.

NOW, SHE'S THE EMPEROR'S TRUTHSAYER. AND PAUL...YOU MUST TELL HER ABOUT YOUR DREAMS.

WHAT'S A GOM JABBAR?

YOU'LL LEARN ABOUT...THE GOM JABBAR SOON ENOUGH. NOW HURRY ALONG. DON'T KEEP REVEREND MOTHER WAITING.

3

DAMN THAT JESSICA! IF ONLY SHE'D BORNE US A GIRL AS SHE WAS ORDERED TO DO!

REVEREND MOTHER, THIS IS PAUL. THE DUKE'S SON.

HE'S A CAUTIOUS ONE, JESSICA.

THUS HE HAS BEEN TAUGHT, YOUR REVERENCE.

TEACHING IS ONE THING. THE BASIC INGREDIENT IS ANOTHER.

LEAVE US. YOU KNOW IT MUST BE DONE.

PAUL, THIS TEST YOU'RE ABOUT TO RECEIVE... IT'S IMPORTANT TO ME.

TEST?

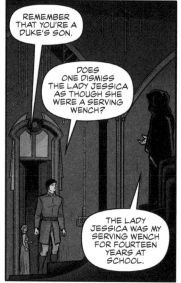

REMEMBER THAT YOU'RE A DUKE'S SON.

DOES ONE DISMISS THE LADY JESSICA AS THOUGH SHE WERE A SERVING WENCH?

THE LADY JESSICA WAS MY SERVING WENCH FOR FOURTEEN YEARS AT SCHOOL.

NOW YOU COME HERE!

USING THE VOICE ON ME! CAN'T... RESIST.

4

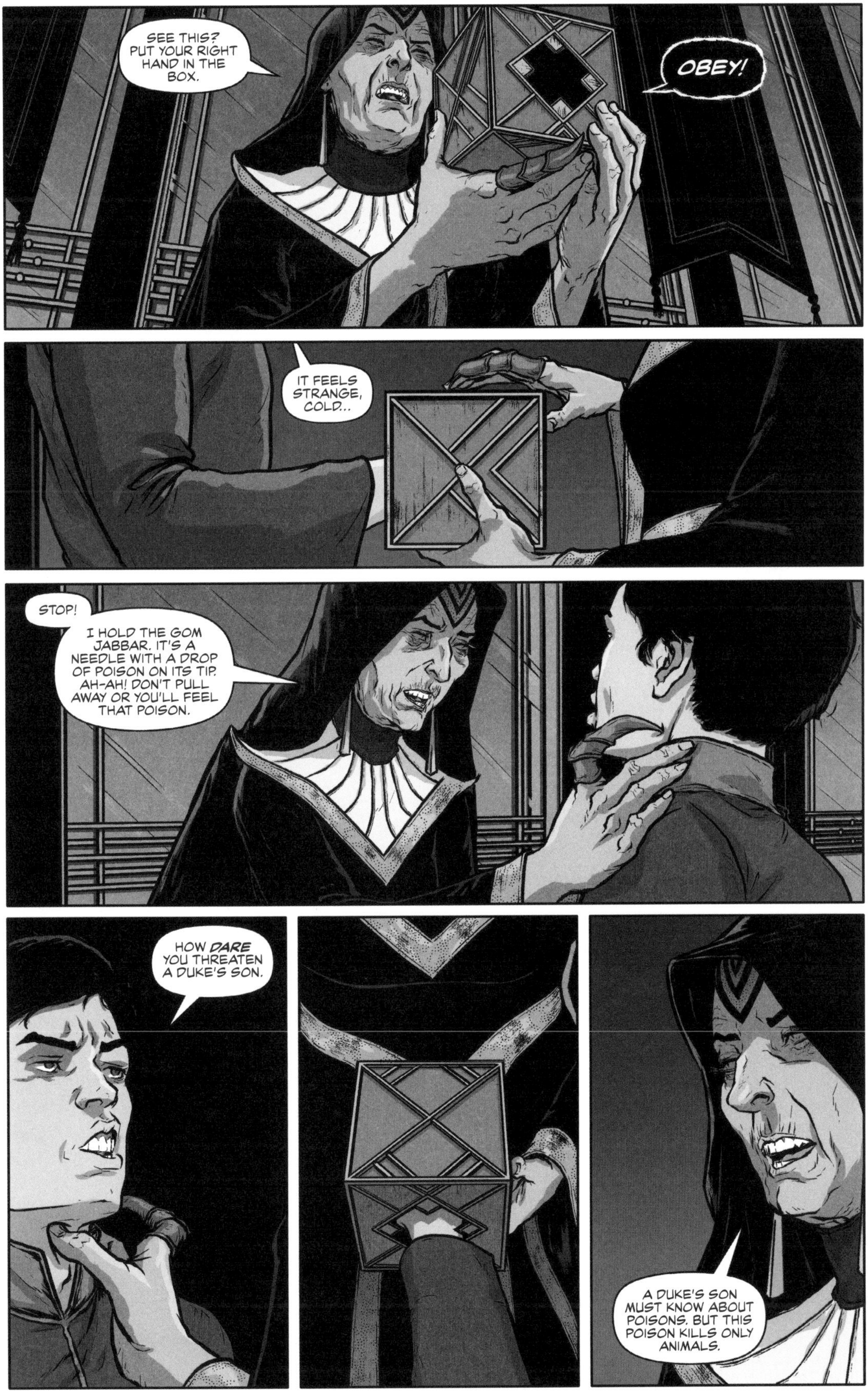
SEE THIS? PUT YOUR RIGHT HAND IN THE BOX.
OBEY!
IT FEELS STRANGE, COLD...
STOP!
I HOLD THE GOM JABBAR. IT'S A NEEDLE WITH A DROP OF POISON ON ITS TIP. AH-AH! DON'T PULL AWAY OR YOU'LL FEEL THAT POISON.
HOW DARE YOU THREATEN A DUKE'S SON.
A DUKE'S SON MUST KNOW ABOUT POISONS. BUT THIS POISON KILLS ONLY ANIMALS.

YOU DARE SUGGEST A DUKE'S SON IS AN ANIMAL?

LET US SAY I SUGGEST YOU MAY BE HUMAN. NOW BE SILENT. IF YOU WITHDRAW YOUR HAND FROM THE BOX, YOU DIE. THAT IS THE ONLY RULE.

KEEP YOUR HAND IN THE BOX AND LIVE. WITHDRAW IT AND DIE.

IF I CALL OUT THERE'LL BE SERVANTS ON YOU IN SECONDS AND YOU'LL DIE.

THEY WILL NOT GET PAST YOUR MOTHER, WHO STANDS GUARD OUTSIDE THAT DOOR. DEPEND ON IT. YOUR MOTHER SURVIVED THIS TEST. NOW IT'S YOUR TURN.

BE HONORED. WE SELDOM ADMINISTER THIS TEST TO MEN-CHILDREN.

I MUST NOT FEAR. FEAR IS THE MIND-KILLER. FEAR IS THE LITTLE-DEATH THAT BRINGS TOTAL OBLITERATION. I WILL FACE MY FEAR.

GET ON WITH IT, OLD WOMAN. WHAT'S IN THE BOX?

I WILL PERMIT IT TO PASS OVER ME AND THROUGH ME. AND WHEN IT HAS GONE PAST I WILL TURN THE INNER EYE TO SEE ITS PATH.

WHERE THE FEAR HAS GONE THERE WILL BE NOTHING.

ONLY I WILL REMAIN.

PAIN. BUT WITHDRAW YOUR HAND, AND FEEL THE PRICK OF THE GOM JABBAR. AND THEN YOUR DEATH WILL BE AS SWIFT AS THE FALL OF THE HEADSMAN'S AX.

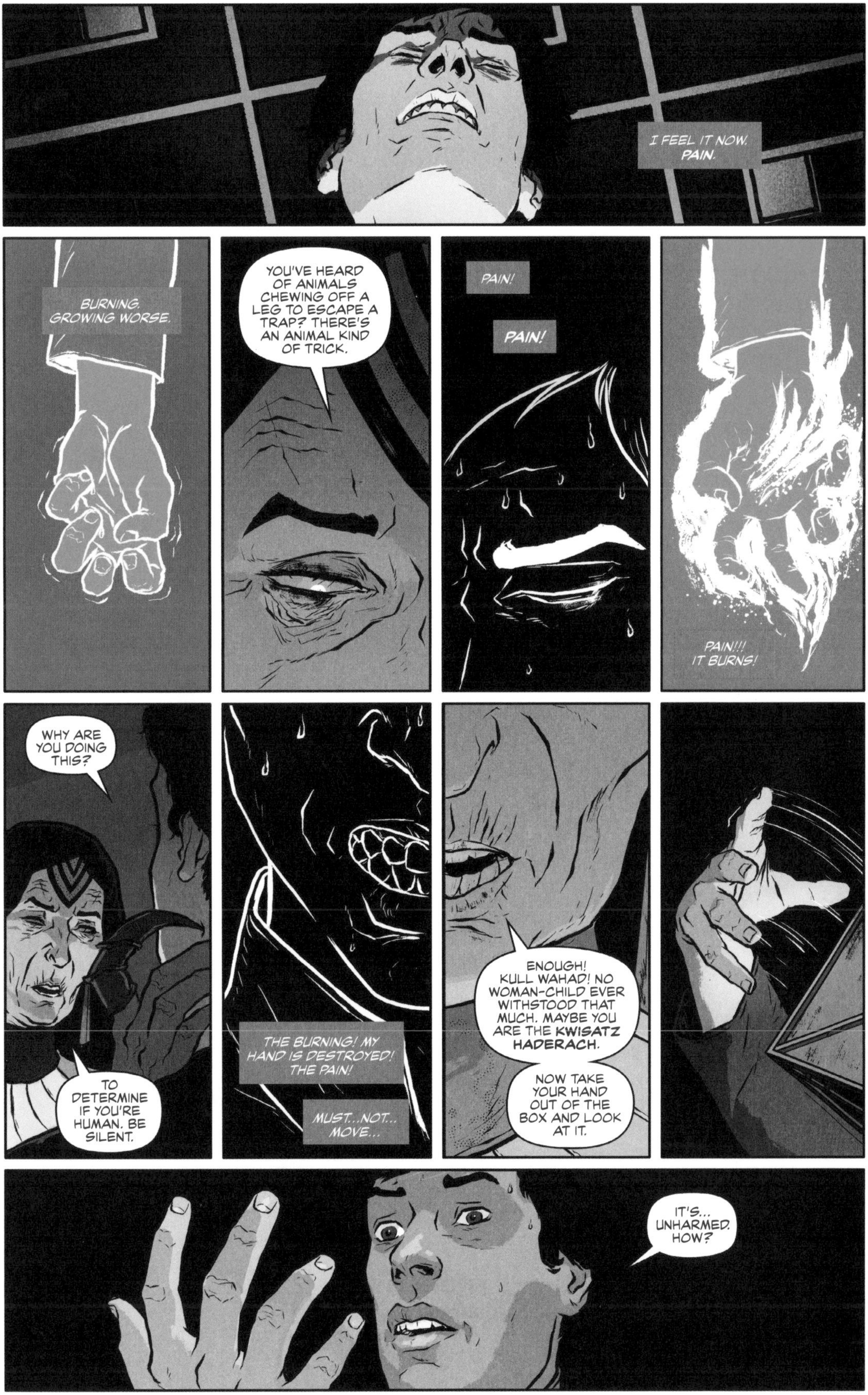

I FEEL IT NOW. PAIN.
BURNING. GROWING WORSE.
YOU'VE HEARD OF ANIMALS CHEWING OFF A LEG TO ESCAPE A TRAP? THERE'S AN ANIMAL KIND OF TRICK.
PAIN!
PAIN!
PAIN!!! IT BURNS!
WHY ARE YOU DOING THIS?
TO DETERMINE IF YOU'RE HUMAN. BE SILENT.
THE BURNING! MY HAND IS DESTROYED! THE PAIN!
MUST...NOT... MOVE...
ENOUGH! KULL WAHAD! NO WOMAN-CHILD EVER WITHSTOOD THAT MUCH. MAYBE YOU ARE THE KWISATZ HADERACH.
NOW TAKE YOUR HAND OUT OF THE BOX AND LOOK AT IT.
IT'S... UNHARMED. HOW?

PAIN BY NERVE INDUCTION. CAN'T GO AROUND MAIMING POTENTIAL HUMANS. A HUMAN CAN OVERRIDE ANY NERVE IN THE BODY.

YOU DID THAT TO MY MOTHER ONCE?

MY SON LIVES! AND HE IS HUMAN. I KNEW HE WAS.

PAUL...?

SOMEDAY, LAD, YOU TOO MAY HAVE TO STAND OUTSIDE A DOOR LIKE THAT. IT TAKES A MEASURE OF DOING.

YOU SAY MAYBE I'M THE...KWISATZ HADERACH. WHAT'S THAT? A HUMAN GOM JABBAR?

THE ONE WHO CAN BE IN MANY PLACES AT ONCE. A GIFTED REVEREND MOTHER CAN LOOK MANY PLACES IN HER MEMORY—IN HER BODY'S MEMORY.

YET THERE'S A PLACE WHERE NONE OF US CAN SEE. IT IS SAID A MAN WILL COME ONE DAY AND FIND HIS INWARD EYE.

HE WILL LOOK WHERE WE CANNOT—INTO BOTH FEMININE AND MASCULINE PASTS.

MANY MEN HAVE TRIED THE DRUG...SO MANY, BUT NONE HAS SUCCEEDED.

THEY TRIED AND FAILED, ALL OF THEM?

OH, NO. THEY TRIED AND DIED.

THE PREPARATIONS CONTINUE AS HOUSE ATREIDES READIES FOR DEPARTURE TO ARRAKIS...

TO TAKE CONTROL OF THE DESERT PLANET FROM HOUSE HARKONNEN.

8

GIEDI PRIME. HOMEWORLD OF HOUSE HARKONNEN.

THERE IT IS, PITER—THE BIGGEST MANTRAP IN ALL HISTORY. AND THE DUKE'S HEADED INTO ITS JAWS.

IS IT NOT A MAGNIFICENT THING THAT I, THE BARON VLADIMIR HARKONNEN, DO?

ASSUREDLY, BARON.

OBSERVE CLOSELY, PITER. AND YOU PAY ATTENTION, TOO, **FEYD-RAUTHA**, MY DARLING. NOT A SPECK OF BLUE ON THE WHOLE GLOBE OF ARRAKIS. TRULY UNIQUE. A SUPERB SETTING FOR A **UNIQUE** VICTORY.

AND TO THINK, THE PADISHAH EMPEROR BELIEVES HE'S GIVEN DUKE LETO ATREIDES YOUR SPICE PLANET. HOW POIGNANT!

WHAT'S THIS, BARON? A MESSAGE CYLINDER—MAYBE THE DUKE HAS RESPONDED!

WELL? WHAT DOES HE SAY?

THE FOOL ANSWERED US, BARON! HE'S MOST UNCOUTH. HE SAYS: "YOUR OFFER OF A MEETING IS **REFUSED**. I HAVE OFTTIMES MET YOUR TREACHERY, AND THIS ALL MEN KNOW."

HE SAYS: "THE ART OF KANLY STILL HAS ADMIRERS IN THE EMPIRE." HE SIGNS IT "DUKE LETO OF ARRAKIS." OH, MY! THIS IS ALMOST TOO RICH!

KANLY, IS IT? VENDETTA.

YOU MADE THE PEACE GESTURE, BARON. THE FORMS HAVE BEEN OBEYED. NEVER HAS REVENGE BEEN MORE BEAUTIFUL.

YOU TALK TOO MUCH, PITER. YOU ARE MY MENTAT ASSASSIN, BUT YOU MAY HAVE OUTLIVED YOUR USEFULNESS. SOMEDAY I WILL HAVE YOU STRANGLED.

AH-AH, BARON! YOU WILL HOLD BACK SO LONG AS I AM USEFUL. YOU WERE NOT ABLE TO DEVISE THIS DELICIOUS SCHEME BY YOURSELF.

DO THEY THINK I'VE NOTHING TO DO EXCEPT LISTEN TO THEIR ARGUMENTS?

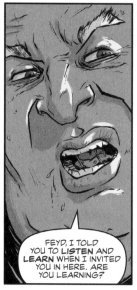

FEYD, I TOLD YOU TO **LISTEN** AND **LEARN** WHEN I INVITED YOU IN HERE. ARE YOU LEARNING?

YES, UNCLE.

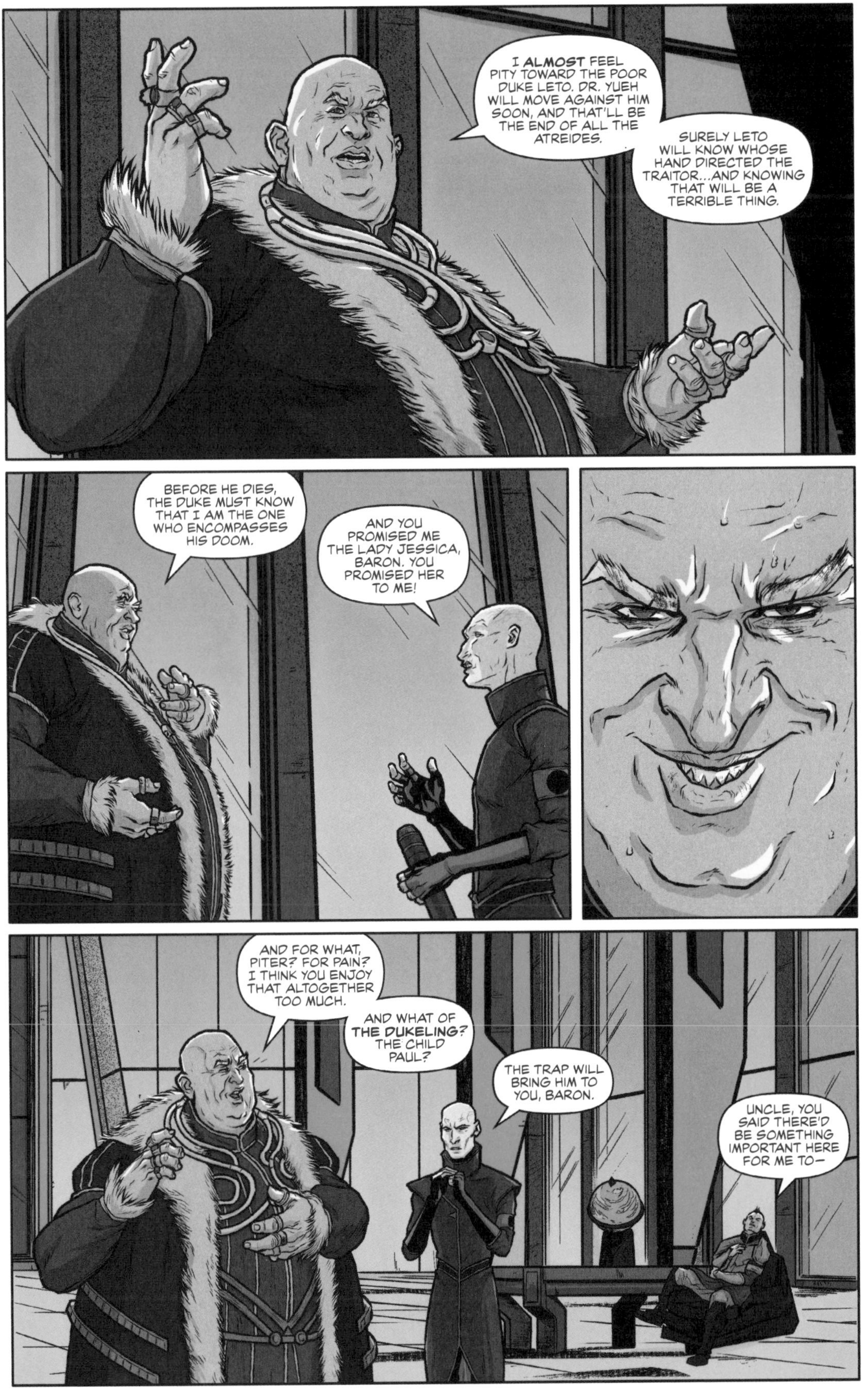
I **ALMOST** FEEL PITY TOWARD THE POOR DUKE LETO. DR. YUEH WILL MOVE AGAINST HIM SOON, AND THAT'LL BE THE END OF ALL THE ATREIDES.
SURELY LETO WILL KNOW WHOSE HAND DIRECTED THE TRAITOR...AND KNOWING THAT WILL BE A TERRIBLE THING.
BEFORE HE DIES, THE DUKE MUST KNOW THAT I AM THE ONE WHO ENCOMPASSES HIS DOOM.
AND YOU PROMISED ME THE LADY JESSICA, BARON. YOU PROMISED HER TO ME!
AND FOR WHAT, PITER? FOR PAIN? I THINK YOU ENJOY THAT ALTOGETHER TOO MUCH.
AND WHAT OF **THE DUKELING?** THE CHILD PAUL?
THE TRAP WILL BRING HIM TO YOU, BARON.
UNCLE, YOU SAID THERE'D BE SOMETHING IMPORTANT HERE FOR ME TO—

MY DARLING FEYD-RAUTHA GROWS IMPATIENT.

I WANT YOU TO LEARN SOMETHING FROM THIS EXCHANGE, TO NOTICE HOW UNSTABLE MY MENTAT MIGHT BE. PITER **MAY** BE A HUMAN COMPUTER, BUT HE IS **STILL** PRONE TO EMOTIONAL OUTBURSTS.

NOW DEMONSTRATE YOUR ABILITIES AS A MENTAT, PITER. OUTLINE FOR MY NEPHEW OUR CAMPAIGN AGAINST HOUSE ATREIDES.

IN A FEW DAYS, THE ENTIRE ATREIDES HOUSEHOLD WILL EMBARK FOR ARRAKIS. THEY WILL OCCUPY ARRAKEEN RATHER THAN OUR CITY OF CARTHAG. THE DUKE'S MENTAT, THUFIR HAWAT, WILL HAVE CONCLUDED RIGHTLY THAT ARRAKEEN IS EASIER TO DEFEND.

THE DUKE AND HIS FAMILY WILL OCCUPY THE RESIDENCY, LATELY THE HOME OF COUNT AND LADY FENRING. WE HAVE MADE ARRANGEMENTS. THERE'LL BE AN ATTEMPT ON THE LIFE OF THE ATREIDES HEIR—AN ATTEMPT WHICH COULD SUCCEED.

THUFIR HAWAT WILL HAVE GUESSED WE HAVE A SPY AMONG THEM, AND AT FIRST HE WILL ASSUME IT'S DR. YUEH—WHO IS, IN TRUTH, OUR AGENT. BUT BECAUSE YUEH HAS THE IMPERIAL CONDITIONING, HE SHOULD **NOT** BE ABLE TO HARM HIS MASTERS, SO HAWAT'S SUSPICIONS WILL TURN **ELSEWHERE**.

LISTEN CAREFULLY, FEYD.

WHERE? WHO?

THE LADY JESSICA!

IS IT NOT SUBLIME? AND WHILE THEIR SUSPICIONS ARE DIVERTED, WE WILL MOVE IN WITH A MAJOR FORCE, STRENGTHENED BY **TWO LEGIONS** OF THE EMPEROR'S SARDAUKAR DISGUISED IN HARKONNEN LIVERY.

SARDAUKAR!

WITHIN A STANDARD YEAR, WE WILL HAVE ARRAKIS BACK AND ALL THE UNIMAGINABLE WEALTH OF SPICE.

AND LOVELIEST OF ALL, THE GREAT HOUSES WILL KNOW THAT THE BARON HAS DESTROYED THE ATREIDES.

AND THE DUKE HIMSELF WILL KNOW. HE WILL KNOW.

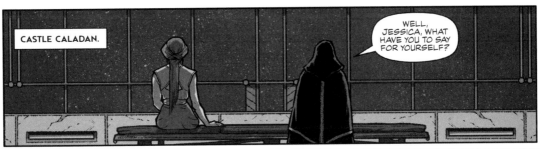

CASTLE CALADAN.

WELL, JESSICA, WHAT HAVE YOU TO SAY FOR YOURSELF?

"I REMEMBER MY OWN ORDEAL, WHEN I WAS TESTED."

"REVEREND MOTHER GAIUS HELEN MOHIAM, PROCTOR SUPERIOR OF THE BENE GESSERIT SCHOOL ON WALLACH IX."

"I REMEMBER THE BOX..."

POOR PAUL...

I ASKED YOU A QUESTION, JESSICA!

WHAT DO YOU WANT ME TO *SAY*? I HAD A SON!

YOU WERE TOLD TO BEAR **ONLY** DAUGHTERS TO THE ATREIDES!

A DAUGHTER COULD HAVE BEEN WED TO A HARKONNEN HEIR AND SEALED THE BREACH.

BUT IT MEANT SO MUCH TO LETO...

SIGH

YOU THOUGHT ONLY OF YOUR DUKE'S DESIRE FOR A SON—AND HIS DESIRES DON'T FIGURE IN THIS.

YOUR PRIDE THOUGHT YOU COULD PRODUCE THE KWISATZ HADERACH!

I SENSED THE POSSIBILITY.

WHAT'S DONE IS DONE.

ALL WE CAN HOPE FOR NOW IS TO PREVENT THIS FROM ERUPTING INTO A GENERAL CONFLAGRATION, TO SALVAGE WHAT WE CAN OF THE KEY BLOODLINES.

I AM A BENE GESSERIT: I EXIST ONLY TO SERVE.

CALL THE BOY IN HERE. HE'S HAD TIME TO THINK AND REMEMBER, AND I MUST ASK ABOUT THESE DREAMS OF HIS.

PAUL, COME IN NOW, PLEASE. THE REVEREND MOTHER NEEDS TO SPEAK WITH YOU.

WHAT DO YOU WANT?

YOUNG MAN, LET US RETURN TO THIS DREAM BUSINESS. DO YOU DREAM EVERY NIGHT? TELL ME ABOUT YOUR DREAMS.

I DREAMED A CAVERN...

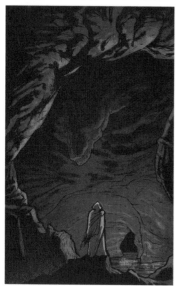

AND WATER...AND A GIRL THERE—VERY SKINNY, WITH BIG EYES. HER EYES ARE ALL BLUE, NO WHITES IN THEM.

MAY I GO NOW?

DON'T YOU WANT TO HEAR WHAT THE REVEREND MOTHER CAN TELL YOU ABOUT THE KWISATZ HADERACH?

SHE SAID THOSE WHO TRIED FOR IT DIED.

YOUR MOTHER SEES THIS POSSIBILITY IN YOU, BUT SHE SEES WITH THE EYES OF A MOTHER. **POSSIBILITY** I SEE, TOO, BUT NO MORE.

YOU THINK I COULD BE THIS KWISATZ HADERACH.

YOU TALK ABOUT ME, BUT YOU HAVEN'T SAID ONE THING ABOUT WHAT WE CAN DO TO HELP MY FATHER. YOU TALK AS THOUGH HE WERE ALREADY **DEAD.** WELL, HE ISN'T!

WE MAY BE ABLE TO SALVAGE YOU. DOUBTFUL, BUT POSSIBLE. BUT FOR YOUR FATHER, **NOTHING.**

I MUST LEAVE NOW. JESSICA, YOU'VE BEEN TRAINING HIM IN **THE WAY.** I'D HAVE DONE THE SAME IN YOUR SHOES, AND DEVIL TAKE THE RULES.

CONTINUE TO GIVE HIM WHAT HE NEEDS. HIS OWN SAFETY REQUIRES THE VOICE.

GOODBYE, YOUNG HUMAN. I HOPE YOU MAKE IT.

BUT IF YOU DON'T—WELL, WE SHALL YET SUCCEED.

ONE WEEK LATER...

THUFIR HAWAT, MENTAT, MASTER OF ASSASSINS. HE HAS SERVED HOUSE ATREIDES FOR THREE GENERATIONS.

AHEM!

HOW MANY TIMES MUST I TELL THAT LAD NEVER TO SETTLE HIMSELF WITH HIS BACK TO A DOOR?

I KNOW, THUFIR HAWAT. I'M SITTING WITH MY BACK TO A DOOR. I HEARD YOU COMING DOWN THE HALL, AND I HEARD YOU OPEN THE DOOR.

THE SOUNDS I MAKE COULD BE IMITATED.

I'D KNOW THE DIFFERENCE.

HE MIGHT AT THAT. THAT WITCH-MOTHER OF HIS IS GIVING HIM THE DEEP TRAINING.

WE'LL ALL BE OUT OF HERE SOON, YOUNG MASTER, AND LIKELY NEVER SEE THE PLACE AGAIN.

TO ARRAKIS. I'VE BEEN STUDYING THE STORMS IN THE DESERT. THEY SOUND PRETTY BAD. WHY DON'T THEY HAVE WEATHER CONTROL?

ARRAKIS HAS SPECIAL PROBLEMS. THE SPACING GUILD WANTS A DREADFUL HIGH PRICE FOR SATELLITE CONTROL.

IS IT AS BAD AS THEY SAY?

NOTHING COULD BE THAT BAD. THE FREMEN TRIBES SURVIVE THERE.

HAVE YOU EVER SEEN A FREMEN, THUFIR?

PERHAPS.

THEY ALL WEAR GREAT FLOWING ROBES, BUT THERE'S LITTLE TO TELL THEM APART FROM THE REST OF THE DESERT PEOPLE.

WATER IS **PRECIOUS** THERE... YOU WILL LEARN A REAL APPRECIATION FOR WATER ON ARRAKIS.

16

THE EMPEROR ORDERED US TO GO, AND SO IT IS OFF TO THE DESERT PLANET FOR US. I LEAVE TODAY FOR ARRAKIS, AND YOU WILL COME IN THE NEXT WAVE.

MEANWHILE, YOU TAKE CARE OF YOURSELF FOR AN OLD MAN WHO'S FOND OF YOU, HEH?

DON'T SIT WITH YOUR BACK TO ANY DOORS, THUFIR!

FREMEN, CORIOLIS STORMS, SPICE PRODUCTION... EVEN GIANT WORMS.

THERE'S TRAINING TO BE DONE, MASTER PAUL.

WELL, GURNEY HALLECK! ARE YOU THE NEW WEAPONS MASTER?

NO SASS FOR YOUR ELDERS TODAY. IF YOU DON'T WANT TO FIGHT, WE'LL HAVE MUSIC INSTEAD.

SINCE YOU'RE SUCH A POOR FIGHTER, LAD, WE'D BEST TEACH YOU THE MUSIC TRADE SO YOUR ENTIRE LIFE ISN'T WASTED.

DUNCAN IDAHO ALREADY GONE TO THE DESERT, THUFIR HAWAT LEAVING. NOTHING TO DO HERE BUT SING.

♫ OH-H-H, THE GALACIAN GIRLS WILL DO IT FOR PEARLS, AND THE ARRAKEEN FOR WATER! ♫

♫ BUT IF YOU DESIRE DAMES LIKE CONSUMING FLAMES, TRY A CALADANIN DAUGHTER! ♫

WITH SUCH POOR SINGING, MAYBE YOU'D BE BETTER OFF FIGHTING.

ZZRT

COMBAT WITH SHIELDS REQUIRES SPECIAL SKILLS. ONE MOVES FAST ON DEFENSE, SLOW ON ATTACK.

SPEED, EXCELLENT, BUT YOU WERE WIDE OPEN FOR AN UNDERHANDED COUNTER WITH A SLIP-TIP.

I SHOULD WHAP YOUR BACKSIDE FOR SUCH CARELESSNESS.

SHWING

THIS IN THE HAND OF AN ENEMY CAN LET OUT YOUR LIFE'S BLOOD!

NOT EVEN IN PLAY DO YOU LET A MAN INSIDE YOUR GUARD WITH **DEATH** IN HIS HAND.

I GUESS I'M NOT IN THE MOOD FOR IT TODAY.

MOOD?!

WHAT HAS MOOD TO DO WITH IT? YOU FIGHT WHEN THE NECESSITY ARISES, NO MATTER THE MOOD!

MOOD'S A THING FOR CATTLE OR MAKING LOVE OR PLAYING THE BALISET. IT'S **NOT** FOR FIGHTING.

I'M SORRY, GURNEY.

NOT SORRY ENOUGH!

NOW GUARD YOURSELF FOR TRUE!

ZZRT

19

WHAT'S GOTTEN INTO GURNEY? HE'S NOT FAKING THIS!

TANG

IS THIS BETRAYAL?

SURELY NOT GURNEY!

I'LL SHOW HIM A TRICK.

ONE MORE STEP, GURNEY.

HAH! IS THIS WHAT YOU SEEK?

GOOD...BUT LOOK DOWN, LAD.

WE'D HAVE JOINED EACH OTHER IN DEATH.

I'LL ADMIT, YOU FOUGHT SOME BETTER WHEN PRESSED TO IT. YOU SEEMED TO GET THE MOOD.

WOULD YOU REALLY HAVE HURT ME?

IF YOU'D FOUGHT ONE WHIT BELOW YOUR ABILITY, I'LL NOT HAVE MY FAVORITE PUPIL FALL TO THE FIRST HARKONNEN WHO HAPPENS ALONG.

NOW, GO! REST UP. WE SAY GOODBYE TO CALADAN SOON.

DR. WELLINGTON YUEH. DOCTOR OF THE SUK SCHOOL.

YOU DO LOOK COMFORTABLE, MASTER PAUL.

CERTIFIED WITH IMPERIAL CONDITIONING, SAFE ENOUGH TO MINISTER EVEN TO THE EMPEROR.

YOU'LL BE HAPPY TO HEAR WE HAVEN'T TIME FOR REGULAR LESSONS TODAY.

YOUR FATHER WILL BE ALONG PRESENTLY.

SUCH A SAD WASTE! I MUST NOT FALTER.

I HAVE LOADED THIS FILMBOOK VIEWER WITH LESSONS ABOUT ARRAKIS. YOU MAY FIND THEM INTERESTING.

WILL THERE BE SOMETHING ABOUT THE FREMEN?

FREMEN? YES, THERE ARE TWO SORTS OF PEOPLE ON ARRAKIS, THE PEOPLE OF THE GRABEN, SINK, AND PAN.

AND THE FREMEN, MUCH MORE RUGGED, MUCH HARDIER. THEIR EYES ARE ENTIRELY BLUE DUE TO THE SATURATION OF **THE SPICE MELANGE** IN THEIR DIET.

AND THE WORMS? I'D LIKE TO STUDY MORE ABOUT THE SANDWORMS.

IT CONTAINS IMAGES OF A SMALL SPECIMEN, ONLY ONE HUNDRED TEN METERS LONG, BUT WORMS OF MORE THAN FOUR HUNDRED METERS HAVE BEEN SIGHTED IN THE DEEP DESERT.

I WOULD LIKE TO GIVE YOU A GIFT, A VERY OLD COPY OF THE ORANGE CATHOLIC BIBLE MADE FOR SPACE TRAVELERS.

IT'S SO SMALL.

BUT EIGHTEEN HUNDRED PAGES LONG, HELD CLOSED BY THE CHARGE. YOU PRESS THE EDGES AND A MAGNIFIER EXPANDS THE PAGES. GO ON, READ A VERSE.

HIS MOTHER WOULD SURELY WONDER AT MY MOTIVES.

"WHAT SENSES DO WE LACK THAT WE CANNOT SEE AND CANNOT HEAR ANOTHER WORLD ALL AROUND US? WHAT IS THERE AROUND US THAT WE CANNOT—"

STOP! STOP, NOT THAT VERSE!

MY POOR WANNA'S FAVORITE VERSE. BEFORE THOSE HARKONNEN ANIMALS...

IS SOMETHING WRONG?

I'M SORRY... THAT WAS...MY... DEAD WIFE'S FAVORITE PASSAGE, NOT THE ONE I INTENDED YOU TO READ. IT BRINGS UP MEMORIES THAT ARE...PAINFUL.

I'M SORRY, I FOUND AN INDENTATION IN THE PAGES.

OF COURSE... MY DEAR WANNA MUST HAVE MARKED IT.

OF ALL VERSES, WHY DID HE HAVE TO PICK THAT ONE?

I MUST BE GOING. KEEP THE BOOK AND READ IT AT YOUR LEISURE, BUT FOR NOW ATTEND TO YOUR STUDIES. YOUR FATHER WILL BE HERE SOON.

DUKE LETO ATREIDES. LEADER OF ONE OF THE GREAT HOUSES OF THE LANDSRAAD.

SOON TO BECOME DUKE OF ARRAKIS, BY COMMAND OF THE PADISHAH EMPEROR SHADDAM IV.

HARD AT WORK, SON? TOMORROW WE LEAVE.

EVERYTHING'S SO...

IT'LL BE GOOD TO GET SETTLED IN OUR NEW HOME, PUT ALL THIS UPSET BEHIND.

WHY DID THE REVEREND MOTHER SAY "FOR THE FATHER, NOTHING"?

WILL ARRAKIS BE AS DANGEROUS AS EVERYONE SAYS?

IT'LL BE DANGEROUS.

THUFIR THINKS ARRAKIS MIGHT BE A HARKONNEN TRAP. THE SPICE OPERATIONS ARE TOO VALUABLE, AND THEY WANT SPICE PRODUCTION TO FAIL AND YOU TO BE BLAMED.

THE HARKONNENS HAVE BEEN STOCKPILING SPICE FOR YEARS. BUT KNOWING WHERE THE TRAP IS—THAT'S THE FIRST STEP IN EVADING IT.

BUT WE MAY HAVE UNEXPECTED ALLIES. THE FREMEN ARE RUTHLESS FIGHTERS, AND UNDERESTIMATED.

THEY HAVE BEEN UNDER THE HARKONNEN YOKE FOR TOO LONG. WE HAVE TO SHOW THEM THAT WE ARE DIFFERENT.

IF WE CAN WIN THE LOYALTY OF THE FREMEN...

I'VE ALREADY SENT DUNCAN IDAHO AMONG THEM AS OUR SECRET REPRESENTATIVE.

THE FRIGATES ARE PREPARING TO DEPART FOR ORBIT AS SOON AS THE GUILD HEIGHLINER ARRIVES. READY YOURSELF, AND REST WELL.

THERE'LL BE NO REST ONCE WE ARRIVE AT ARRAKIS.

CALADAN... SO MUCH WATER.

WILL WE FEEL IT WHEN THE HOLTZMAN ENGINES FOLD SPACE?

WILL THE NAVIGATOR GUIDE US SAFELY?

DON'T WORRY, PAUL. WE'LL BE SAFE.

UNTIL WE REACH ARRAKIS...

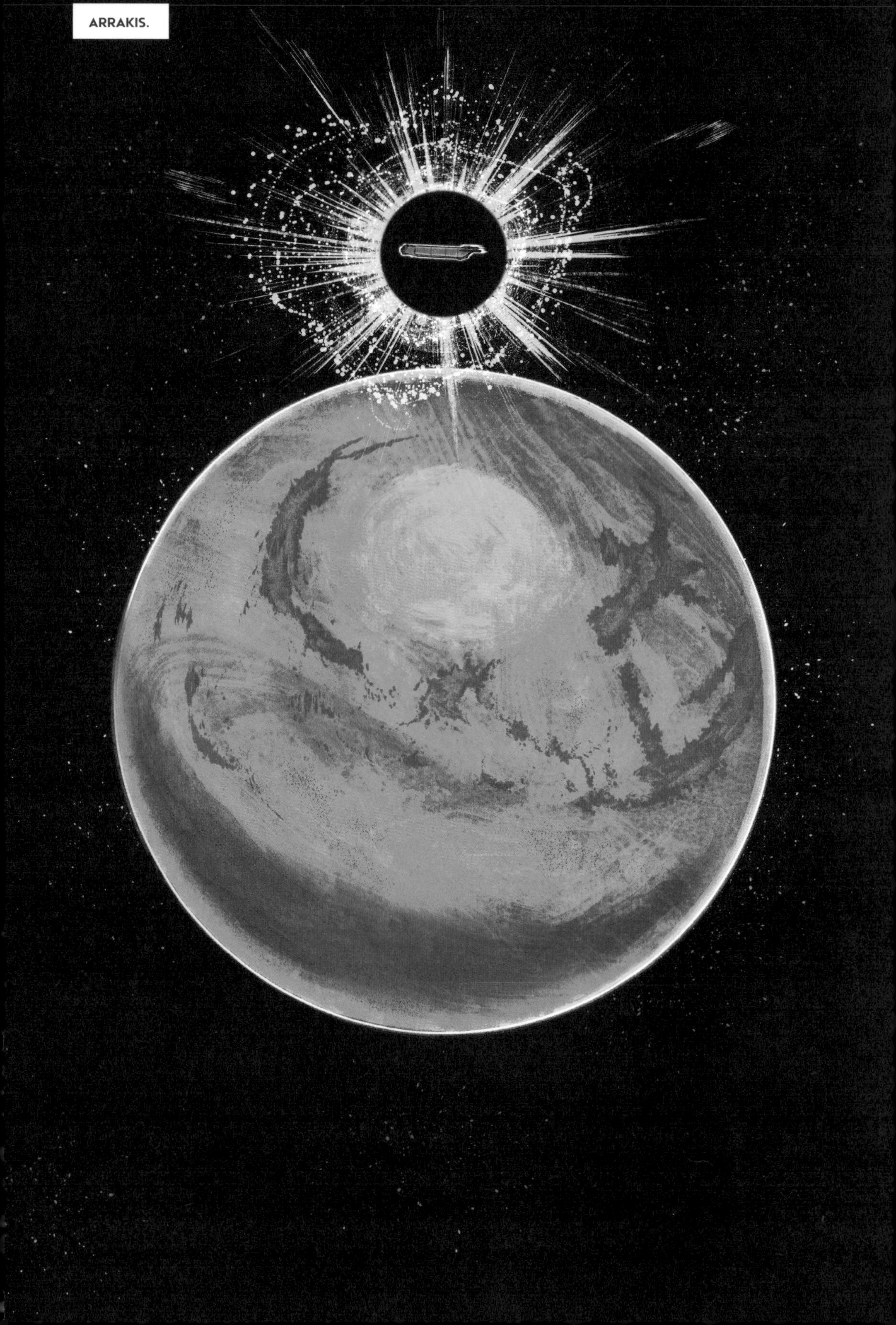
ARRAKIS.

THE CITY OF ARRAKEEN, NEW CAPITAL OF HOUSE ATREIDES.

FAR FROM CARTHAG, FORMER GOVERNMENTAL SEAT UNDER HARKONNEN RULE.

ARRAKEEN IS PROTECTED FROM THE DEEP DESERT— AND SANDWORMS—BY THE TOWERING SHIELD WALL.

THE ARRAKEEN RESIDENCY, FORMER HOME OF COUNT FENRING—EMPEROR SHADDAM'S PROXY ON ARRAKIS—AND HIS WIFE, LADY FENRING.

DUKE LETO HAS CLAIMED THE RESIDENCY AS HIS NEW HEADQUARTERS.

OUR NEW HOME...SO DIFFERENT.

"SO FAR AWAY, CALADAN..."

LETO'S FATHER, THE OLD DUKE...A HARD MAN, LONG DEAD NOW.

AND THE BEAST THAT KILLED HIM...

HERE WE ARE!

WHAT MADE ME OPEN THESE TWO CRATES FIRST? WHAT *MEANING* DO I DRAW FROM THAT?

I THOUGHT YOU MIGHT HAVE LOST YOURSELF IN THIS HIDEOUS PLACE. IT'S A DIRTY, DUSTY LITTLE GARRISON TOWN, BUT WE'LL CHANGE THAT.

I LEAVE YOU TO SET UP OUR NEW HOUSEHOLD. THUFIR HAWAT IS SEEING TO ALL OUR SECURITY.

WHERE'S PAUL?

SOMEPLACE AROUND THE HOUSE TAKING HIS LESSONS WITH YUEH.

WHERE WERE YOU GOING TO HANG THESE? I WANT THEM IN THE DINING HALL.

NO! MY LORD, IF YOU'D ONLY...

IN THE DINING HALL. THAT IS MY COMMAND. IT IS PART OF MY ANCESTRAL DIGNITY.

YES, MY LORD.

AND DON'T GO ALL COLD AND FORMAL WITH ME. YOU MAY CHOOSE TO DINE IN YOUR PRIVATE ROOMS WHENEVER YOU WISH, *EXCEPT* FOR OFFICIAL OCCASIONS.

HAWAT HAS ALREADY INSTALLED **POISON SNOOPERS** IN THE MAIN DINING HALL, AND HE WILL INCLUDE ONE IN YOUR ROOMS.

HE HAS ALSO CLEARED THE LOCALS WE HAVE ENGAGED ON STAFF. THEY ARE ALL FREMEN. HE SAYS THEY ARE TRUSTWORTHY.

CAN ANYONE FROM THIS PLACE BE TRULY SAFE?

ANYONE WHO HATES THE HARKONNENS. YOU MAY EVEN WANT TO KEEP THE HEAD HOUSEKEEPER, THE SHADOUT MAPES.

HAWAT SPEAKS HIGHLY OF HER ON THE BASIS OF DUNCAN IDAHO'S REPORT.

THEY'RE CONVINCED SHE WANTS TO SERVE— SPECIFICALLY, THAT SHE WANTS TO SERVE **YOU.**

ME?

THE FREMEN HAVE LEARNED THAT YOU'RE BENE GESSERIT. THERE ARE LEGENDS HERE ABOUT THE BENE GESSERIT.

DOES THIS MEAN DUNCAN WAS SUCCESSFUL? WILL THE FREMEN BE OUR ALLIES?

I HEAR THEIR RAIDS CAUSED A GREAT AMOUNT OF DAMAGE TO HARKONNEN OPERATIONS.

THERE'S NOTHING DEFINITE. THEY WISH TO OBSERVE US FOR A WHILE. BUT MAYBE...

THERE'S A DEEP **STRENGTH** IN THE FREMEN. I THINK THEY'LL BE EVERYTHING WE NEED.

IT'S A DANGEROUS GAMBLE.

LET'S NOT GO INTO THAT AGAIN.

THIS PLANET'S **INFESTED** WITH HARKONNEN INTRIGUES.

I'LL EAT IN THE OFFICERS' MESS AT THE FIELD. SO MUCH SECURITY TO OVERSEE, AND THUFIR CAN'T HANDLE IT ALL. **DON'T** EXPECT ME UNTIL VERY LATE.

DAMN YOU! DAMN YOU! DAMN YOU!

EXCUSE ME, MY LADY. I AM CALLED THE SHADOUT MAPES, NOBLE BORN.

WHAT ARE YOUR ORDERS?

OH...MAPES. I'VE BEEN EXPECTING YOU. YOU MAY REFER TO ME AS "MY LADY."

I'M **NOT** NOBLE BORN. I'M THE BOUND CONCUBINE OF THE DUKE LETO.

CONCUBINE... THERE'S A WIFE, THEN?

THERE IS NOT, NOR HAS THERE EVER BEEN.

I AM THE DUKE'S ONLY... COMPANION, THE MOTHER OF HIS DESIGNATED HEIR.

WHAT IS THAT CALL?

I HEARD IT AS WE DROVE THROUGH THE STREETS THIS MORNING.

ONLY A WATER-SELLER, MY LADY. BUT YOU'VE NO NEED TO INTEREST YOURSELF IN SUCH AS THEY.

YOU WILL NEVER WANT FOR WATER IN THE RESIDENCE. I DON'T EVEN HAVE TO WEAR MY STILLSUIT HERE!

THEY SAY YOU ARE A BENE GESSERIT, MY LADY.

JUST AS THE LEGEND SAYS...

AH, THE BENE GESSERIT'S MISSIONARIA PROTECTIVA HAS SPREAD THE LEGENDS HERE, TO PROTECT SISTERS LIKE MYSELF...

YES, AND I KNOW MANY THINGS.

I KNOW THAT YOU HAVE BORNE CHILDREN, THAT YOU HAVE LOST LOVED ONES, THAT YOU HAVE HIDDEN IN FEAR, AND THAT YOU HAVE DONE VIOLENCE AND WILL YET DO **MORE** VIOLENCE.

I KNOW MANY THINGS.

I...I MEANT NO OFFENSE, MY LADY!

I MUST PRESS MY ADVANTAGE, USE MY POWERS OF OBSERVATION. I MUST MAKE HER AFRAID...

I KNOW YOU CAME PREPARED FOR VIOLENCE WITH A WEAPON IN YOUR BODICE.

BEWARE THE ANSWERS YOU MAY FIND.

MY LADY! THE WEAPON WAS SENT AS A GIFT TO YOU SHOULD YOU PROVE TO BE THE ONE.

DO YOU KNOW THIS, MY LADY?

I MUST ANSWER CORRECTLY...THINK OF RUMORS, LEGENDS.

IT IS A CRYSKNIFE, A BLADE THAT HAS NEVER BEEN SEEN OFF-PLANET.

SAY IT NOT LIGHTLY. DO YOU KNOW ITS MEANING?

ANOTHER TEST. THINK OF THE LANGUAGE, THE DERIVATIVE CHAKOBSA WORDS...SHE IS FREMEN.

IT IS A... MAKER.

31

EEEEEEE!

DID YOU THINK THAT I, KNOWING THE MYSTERIES OF THE GREAT MOTHER, WOULD NOT KNOW THE MAKER?

MY LADY, WHEN ONE HAS LIVED WITH PROPHECY FOR SO LONG, THE MOMENT OF REVELATION IS A SHOCK.

TAKE THE WATER OF MY LIFE! A CRYSKNIFE MUST NOT BE SHEATHED UNBLOODED.

A SCRATCH IS ENOUGH, MAPES.

YOU ARE OURS.

YOU ARE THE ONE.

WHO SEES THAT KNIFE MUST BE CLEANSED OR SLAIN! YOU KNOW THAT, MY LADY!

I KNOW IT NOW...

NOW THE THING MUST TAKE ITS COURSE. IT CANNOT BE HURRIED.

GOOD AFTERNOON, DR. YUEH. WHERE'S PAUL?

YOUR SON GREW TIRED, JESSICA.

I SENT HIM INTO THE NEXT ROOM TO REST.

FORGIVE ME, MY LADY!

MY THOUGHTS WERE FAR AWAY... I...DID NOT MEAN TO BE FAMILIAR. TO USE YOUR NAME LIKE THAT...I...

WE'VE KNOWN EACH OTHER SIX YEARS, WELLINGTON.

IT'S LONG PAST TIME WE SHOULD HAVE DROPPED FORMALITIES BETWEEN US—IN PRIVATE.

I BELIEVE IT'S WORKED. NOW SHE WON'T LOOK FOR OTHER ANSWERS TO MY ODD BEHAVIOR.

I'M AFRAID I WAS WOOLGATHERING, STARING AT THE PEOPLE OUT THERE. THEY'VE NEVER KNOWN ANYTHING OTHER THAN HARKONNENS.

THOSE PALM TREES...THE WAY THEY LOOK AT THEM.

SOME WITH ENVY, SOME WITH HATE. SOME WITH HOPE.

"MY LADY, THEY LOOK AT THOSE TREES AND THEY THINK, 'THERE ARE ONE HUNDRED OF US.'"

"ONE DATE PALM REQUIRES FORTY LITERS OF WATER A DAY. A MAN REQUIRES BUT EIGHT LITERS."

"A PALM, THEN, EQUALS FIVE MEN. THERE ARE TWENTY PALMS OUT THERE—ONE HUNDRED MEN."

"BUT SOME OF THOSE PEOPLE LOOK AT THE TREES HOPEFULLY, WELLINGTON."

"THEY BUT HOPE DATES WILL FALL, MY LADY."

YOU ARE TOO CRITICAL.

THERE'S HOPE AS WELL AS DANGER HERE.

THE SPICE PROFITS COULD MAKE US RICH. AND WITH A FAT TREASURY, WE CAN **MAKE** THIS WORLD INTO WHATEVER WE WISH.

WOULD IT DISTURB PAUL IF I LOOKED IN ON HIM?

NOT AT ALL. I GAVE HIM A SEDATIVE.

WHAT DELICIOUS ABANDON IN THE SLEEP OF A CHILD.

IF ONLY ADULTS COULD RELAX LIKE THAT. WHERE DO WE LOSE IT?

WHY DID WANNA NEVER GIVE ME CHILDREN? WAS THERE SOME BENE GESSERIT **REASON**? WAS SHE, PERHAPS, INSTRUCTED TO SERVE A DIFFERENT PURPOSE?

MY **POOR** WANNA...THOSE HARKONNEN ANIMALS!

IS SOMETHING WRONG?

JUST THIS PLACE...THE WHOLE PLANET'S A HARKONNEN TRAP.

THE WAY YOU SAY HARKONNEN. EVEN MY DUKE'S VOICE DOESN'T CARRY THAT WEIGHT OF VENOM WHEN HE USES THE HATED NAME.

I DIDN'T KNOW YOU HAD PERSONAL REASONS TO HATE THEM, WELLINGTON.

I'VE AROUSED HER SUSPICIONS! NOW I MUST USE EVERY TRICK MY WANNA TAUGHT ME. THERE'S ONLY ONE SOLUTION: TELL THE TRUTH AS FAR AS I CAN.

YOU DIDN'T KNOW THAT MY WIFE, MY WANNA...THE HARKONNENS...I AM SORRY. I'M UNABLE TO TALK ABOUT IT.

FORGIVE ME, I DID NOT MEAN TO OPEN AN OLD WOUND.

WE BOTH HAVE REASON TO HATE THE HARKONNENS. THERE'LL BE MUCH BLOODSHED SOON. THE BARON WON'T REST UNTIL HE'S DEAD OR MY DUKE DESTROYED.

THE OLD FEUD...IT WILL TAKE MORE THAN A TRAP TO CATCH THE DUKE LETO.

YES, I SINCERELY BELIEVE SO.

NOW LET US LEAVE PAUL TO HIS SLEEP...

HE IS HIDING SOMETHING, I CAN TELL. WHAT DOESN'T HE WANT ME TO KNOW?

35

SO MUCH TO EXPLORE IN THIS NEW PLACE, SO MANY MYSTERIES. NO TIME FOR SLEEP...

IT WAS EASY TO PALM DR. YUEH'S SLEEPING PILL...

SUCH INTRICATE CARVINGS ON THE HEADBOARD. THEY HIDE CONTROLS FOR THE ROOM, THE LIGHTS, THE TEMPERATURE...

AND THE LEAPING FISH CARVED INTO THE WOOD. WHEN HAS ARRAKIS EVER KNOWN FISH?

OR WOOD, FOR THAT MATTER...

I WANT TO SEE WHAT THIS PLACE HOLDS. IF I SLIP OUT WITHOUT ASKING, I HAVEN'T DISOBEYED ORDERS...

AND I WILL STAY IN THE HOUSE, WHERE IT'S SAFE.

WE BOTH HAVE REASON TO HATE THE HARKONNENS. THERE'LL BE MUCH BLOODSHED SOON.

THE BARON WON'T REST UNTIL HE'S DEAD OR MY DUKE DESTROYED.

THE OLD FEUD... IT WILL TAKE MORE THAN A TRAP TO CATCH THE DUKE LETO.

YES, I SINCERELY BELIEVE SO. NOW LET US LEAVE PAUL TO HIS SLEEP...

FASCINATING ITEMS LEFT BEHIND HERE.

THIS CABINET, THE HANDLES LOOK LIKE ORNITHOPTER THRUST BARS, AND THE CARVED HEADBOARD...

ALMOST AS IF THIS ROOM WAS *DESIGNED* TO ENTICE ME.

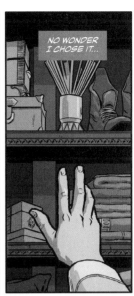

NO WONDER I CHOSE IT...

WHAT'S THAT SOUND?

STEALTHY... A TRAP?

CLICK

VZZZZZZ

HUNTER-SEEKER!

VZZZZZZ

ASSASSINATION WEAPON. IT FINDS ITS TARGET, BURROWS INTO FLESH.

VZZZZZZ

MUST NOT MOVE. NOT EVEN A FLICKER. IT SENSES MOTION.

VZZZZZZ

I CAN'T CRY OUT. I'D BE DEAD BEFORE ANYONE COULD COME.

I HAVE ONLY MY WITS TO FIGHT IT.

I MUST TRY TO GRAB IT. THE SUSPENSOR FIELD WILL MAKE IT SLIPPERY ON THE BOTTOM. I MUST GRIP TIGHTLY...

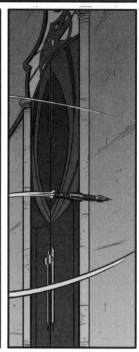

WHO IS OPERATING THAT THING? IT HAS TO BE SOMEONE NEAR.

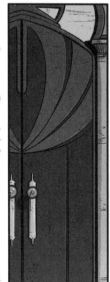

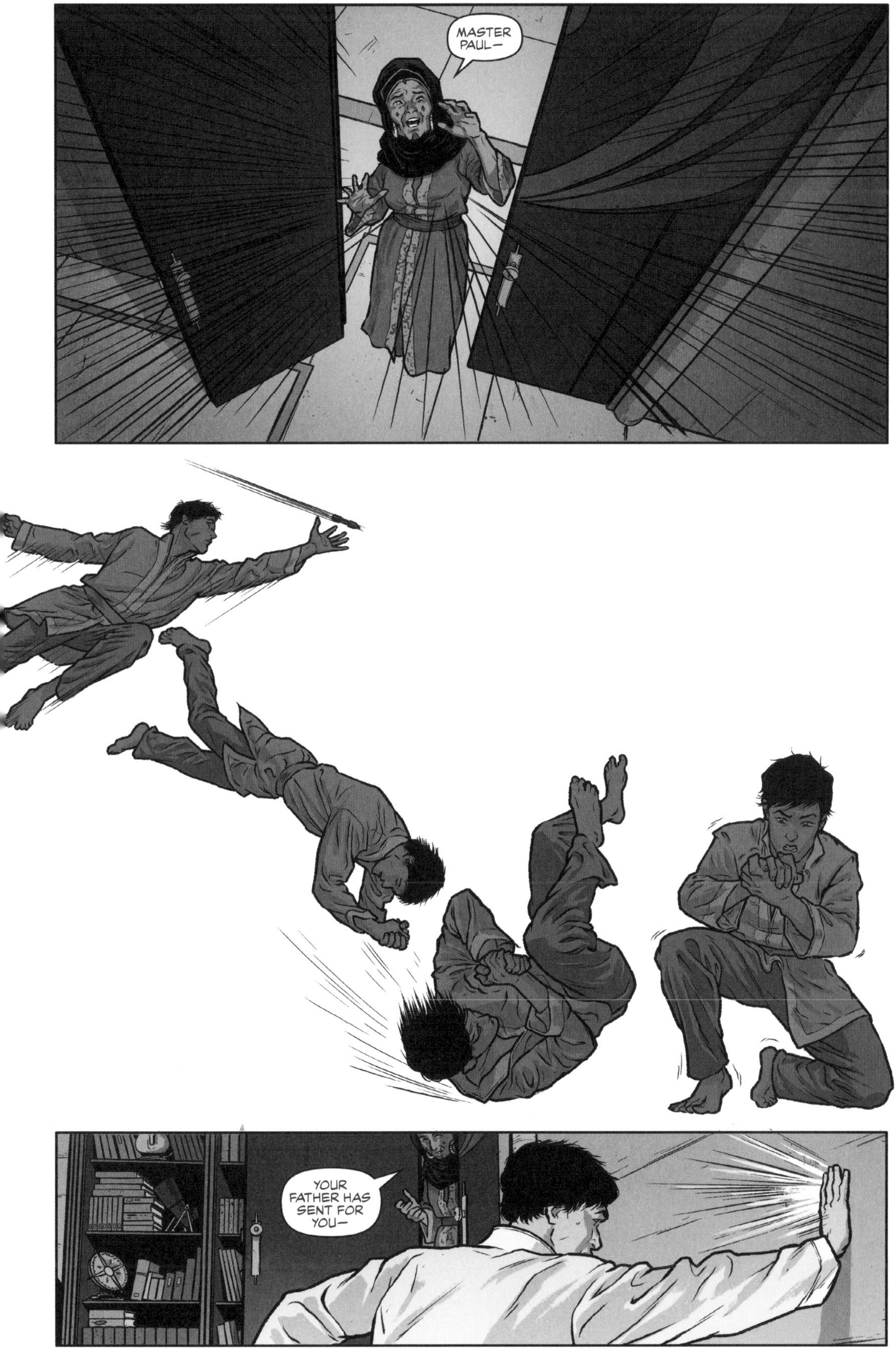
MASTER PAUL—
YOUR FATHER HAS SENT FOR YOU—

A HUNTER-SEEKER. SOMEONE SENT IT...

I'VE HEARD OF SUCHLIKE. IT WOULD'VE KILLED ME, NOT SO?

I WAS ITS TARGET. IT ONLY CAME FOR YOU BECAUSE YOU WERE MOVING.

THEN YOU SAVED MY LIFE.

GO TO MY FATHER'S MEN.

TELL THEM I'VE CAUGHT A HUNTER-SEEKER IN THE HOUSE AND THEY'RE TO SPREAD OUT AND FIND THE OPERATOR. HE'S SURE TO BE A STRANGER AMONG US.

WHO COULD IT BE? WE MUST FIND THE OPERATOR OF THIS THING.

BEFORE I DO YOUR BIDDING, I MUST CLEANSE THE WAY BETWEEN US. YOU'VE PUT A WATER BURDEN ON ME, AND WE FREMEN PAY OUR DEBTS.

SO I WILL TELL YOU THIS. IT IS KNOWN TO US THAT YOU HAVE A TRAITOR IN YOUR MIDST. BUT I KNOW NO MORE THAN THAT.

WHERE IS MY MOTHER? I MUST SPEAK WITH HER.

SHE IS IN THE WEIRDING ROOM, A SPECIAL PLACE OF LADY FENRING'S. I WILL TELL YOU THE WAY.

SO MANY STRANGE ROOMS IN THE RESIDENCY. THIS PLACE IS A LABYRINTH.

AN OVAL DOOR? HOW UNUSUAL.

FAINT SPECKS ON THE STAIRS. DIRT? REAL DIRT?

NO HANDLE ON THE DOOR, JUST A FAINT DEPRESSION.

SURELY IT CAN'T BE A PALM LOCK? IT WOULD HAVE TO BE SPECIFICALLY KEYED...

THUFIR HAWAT RAN HIS SECURITY THROUGH THE ENTIRE RESIDENCY. HE CERTIFIED THIS PLACE...

VMMP

AN AIRLOCK? A SECOND CHAMBER? WHY AN AIRLOCK IN A HOUSE?

SPECIAL CLIMATE!

HERE ON ARRAKIS, THE MEASURES TAKEN TO PRESERVE A DELICATE CLIMATE...

A WET-PLANET CONSERVATORY, HERE!

SO MANY PLANTS, SO MANY SPECIES NEVER SEEN ON THIS DESERT PLANET.

THE SOUND OF RUNNING WATER. SO ALIEN HERE...

WATER EVERYWHERE IN THIS ROOM—ON A PLANET WHERE WATER IS THE MOST PRECIOUS JUICE OF LIFE.

WHO BUILT THIS PLACE? SUCH A DANGEROUS EXTRAVAGANCE!

WAS IT MY LETO, TO SURPRISE ME?

NO, NOT LETO.

A MESSAGE?

To the Lady Jessica—

May this place give you as much pleasure as it has given me. Please permit the room to convey a lesson we learned from the same teachers: the proximity of a desirable thing tempts one to overindulgence. On that path lies danger.

My kindest wishes,

Margot Lady Fenring

43

MARGOT FENRING, WIFE OF COUNT FENRING, THE PREVIOUS RESIDENTS HERE.

MARGOT WAS ALSO A BENE GESSERIT, AND THE CODING IN THIS MESSAGE IS UNMISTAKABLE: DANGER.

THERE'S A HIDDEN MESSAGE... SOMEWHERE.

AH!

"Your son and Duke are in immediate danger.

"A bedroom has been designed to attract your son. The H loaded it with death traps to be discovered, leaving one that may escape detection."

"I do not know the exact nature of the menace, but it has something to do with a bed. The threat to your Duke involves defection of a trusted companion or lieutenant."

"The H plan to give you as gift to a minion. To the best of my knowledge, this conservatory is safe. Forgive that I cannot tell more. My sources are few as my Count is not in the pay of the H. In haste, MF."

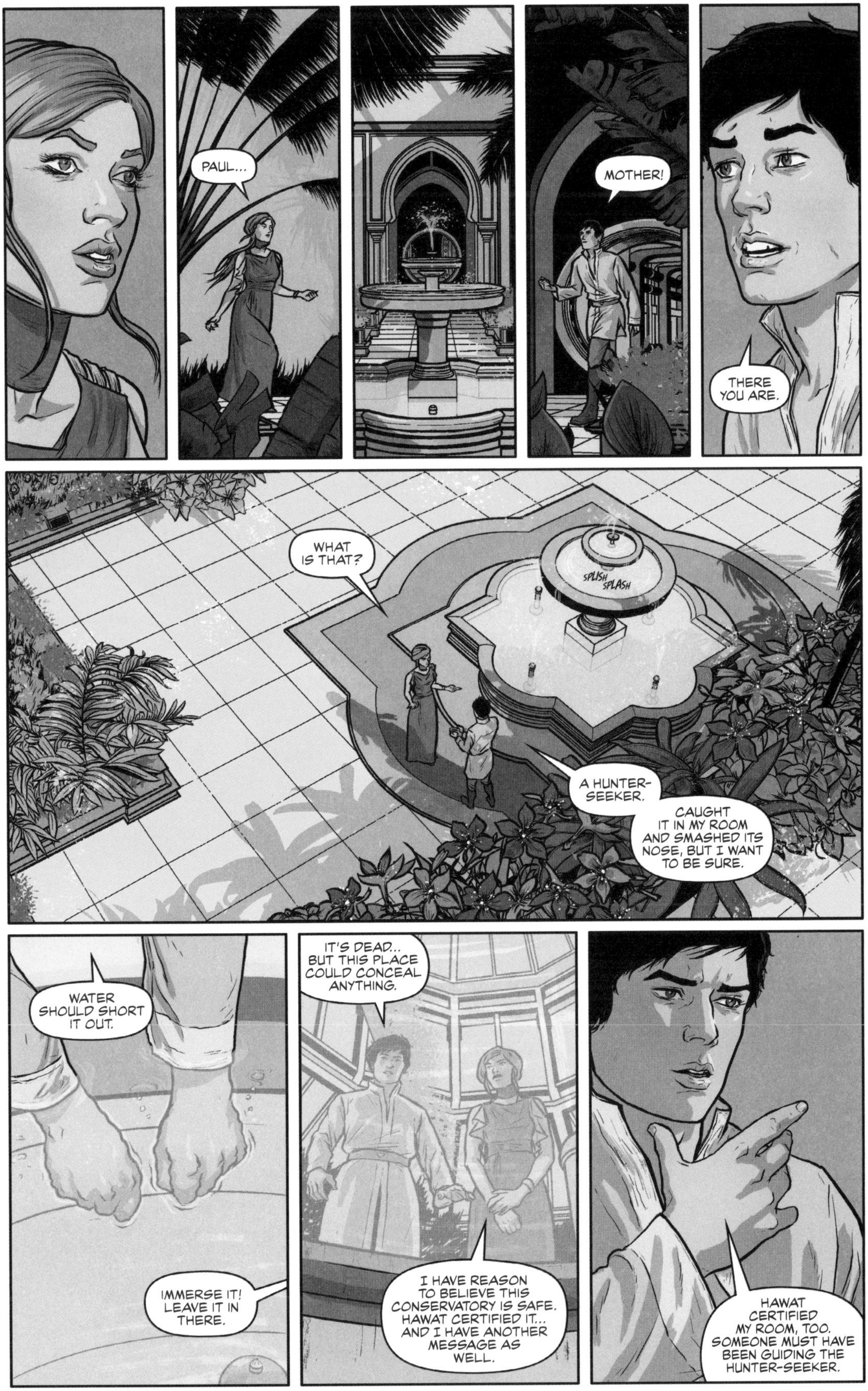
PAUL...
MOTHER!
THERE YOU ARE.
WHAT IS THAT?
SPLISH SPLASH
A HUNTER-SEEKER.
CAUGHT IT IN MY ROOM AND SMASHED ITS NOSE, BUT I WANT TO BE SURE.
WATER SHOULD SHORT IT OUT.
IMMERSE IT! LEAVE IT IN THERE.
IT'S DEAD... BUT THIS PLACE COULD CONCEAL ANYTHING.
I HAVE REASON TO BELIEVE THIS CONSERVATORY IS SAFE. HAWAT CERTIFIED IT... AND I HAVE ANOTHER MESSAGE AS WELL.
HAWAT CERTIFIED MY ROOM, TOO. SOMEONE MUST HAVE BEEN GUIDING THE HUNTER-SEEKER.

THERE YOU ARE, MASTER PAUL.

WE FOUND A CAIRN IN THE CELLAR AND CAUGHT A MAN IN IT. HE HAD A SEEKER CONSOLE.

HE MUST HAVE SEALED HIMSELF IN THERE FOR MORE THAN A MONTH, BEFORE THE HARKONNENS LEFT. A TRAP...

I'LL WANT TO TAKE PART IN THE INTERROGATION.

SORRY, MY LADY, WE MESSED HIM UP CATCHING HIM. HE DIED.

SEND WORD TO MY FATHER THAT WE'LL BE DELAYED.

YES, SIR. I'LL MOUNT A GUARD OUTSIDE THE DOOR TO KEEP YOU SAFE.

HAWAT ENSURED THIS WING WAS SAFE. HOW COULD HE MISS SUCH THINGS?

THUFIR HAWAT HAS SERVED THREE GENERATIONS OF ATREIDES WITH HONOR. BUT HE IS OLD.

IS HE THE TRAITOR?

I'M AFRAID WE CAN'T TRUST **ANYONE** FOR NOW. BE VERY CAREFUL...

AFTER I SAVED HER LIFE, THE SHADOUT MAPES REVEALED THAT SHE KNOWS WE HAVE A TRAITOR AMONG US, BUT SHE DOESN'T KNOW **WHO** IT IS.

AND LADY FENRING IS ALSO A BENE GESSERIT. SHE LEFT ME THIS WARNING, HIDDEN ON THE LEAF.

MY FATHER MUST LEARN OF THIS AT ONCE.

TELL HIM IN PERSON; TRUST NO MESSENGER, NO TRANSMITTER.

THERE, LOOK—A SIGNAL! SOMEONE IS FLASHING A MESSAGE.

THERE IS TREACHERY EVERYWHERE...

ALL CLEAR.

TIME TO BE GETTING THE YOUNG MASTER TO HIS FATHER.

ARRAKEEN
SPACEPORT.

THIS TERRIBLE PLACE IS NOW MINE, BY THE EMPEROR'S COMMAND. DOES THAT FOOL ANYONE?

THE ANNOUNCEMENTS HAVE GONE OUT EVERYWHERE.

"OUR SUBLIME PADISHAH EMPEROR HAS CHARGED ME TO TAKE POSSESSION OF THIS PLANET AND END ALL DISPUTE."

THERE IS HARKONNEN TREACHERY EVERYWHERE.

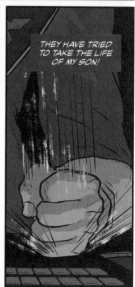

THEY HAVE TRIED TO TAKE THE LIFE OF MY SON!

THAT'LL BE THE LAST OF THE TROOPS ARRIVING.

GURNEY HALLECK WILL BE WITH THEM. IS THERE ANY WORD WHEN PAUL WILL BE ESCORTED OUT HERE TO THE FIELD?

STILL DELAYED, SIR.

THEY HAVE TRIED TO TAKE THE LIFE OF MY SON!

I HOPE THEY'RE KEEPING HIM SAFE.

I WILL NEVER SEE CALADAN AGAIN. IF EVER PAUL IS TO HAVE A HOME, THIS MUST BE IT.

HE MUST FIND SOMETHING HERE THAT WILL *INSPIRE* HIM.

I AM GOING DOWN TO MEET THE NEW ARRIVALS.

FEW OF THEM WANT TO BE HERE. I MUST MAKE THEM UNDERSTAND HOW IMPORTANT IT IS.

HOW MANY G'S DOES THIS PLACE PULL? FEELS HEAVY.

NINE-TENTHS OF A G BY THE BOOK.

ME FOR A HOT SHOWER AND A SOFT BED!

HAVEN'T YOU HEARD, STUPID? NO SHOWERS DOWN HERE. YOU SCRUB YOUR ASS WITH SAND.

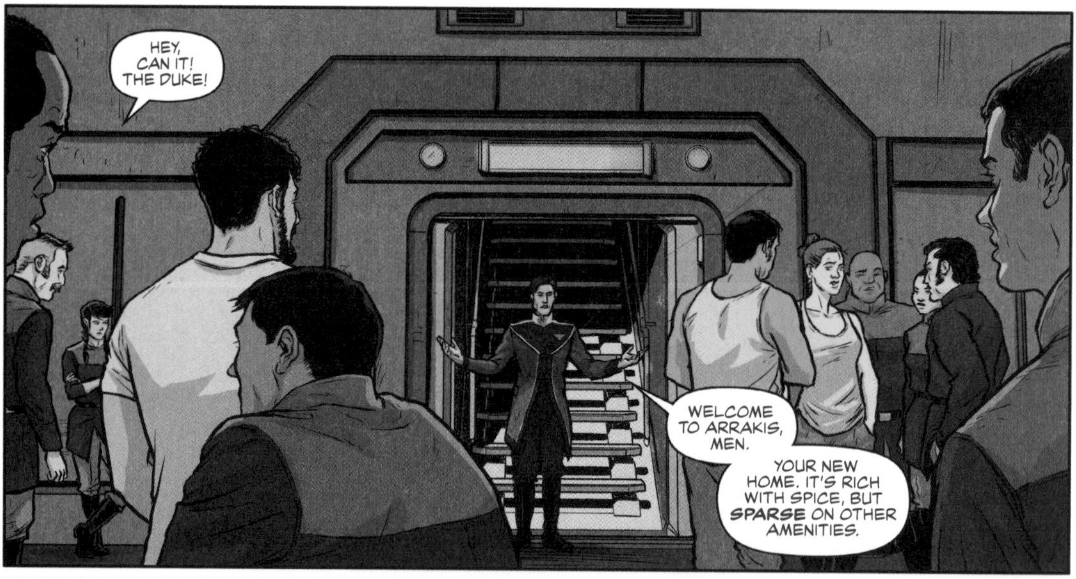
HEY, CAN IT! THE DUKE!
WELCOME TO ARRAKIS, MEN.
YOUR NEW HOME. IT'S RICH WITH SPICE, BUT **SPARSE** ON OTHER AMENITIES.

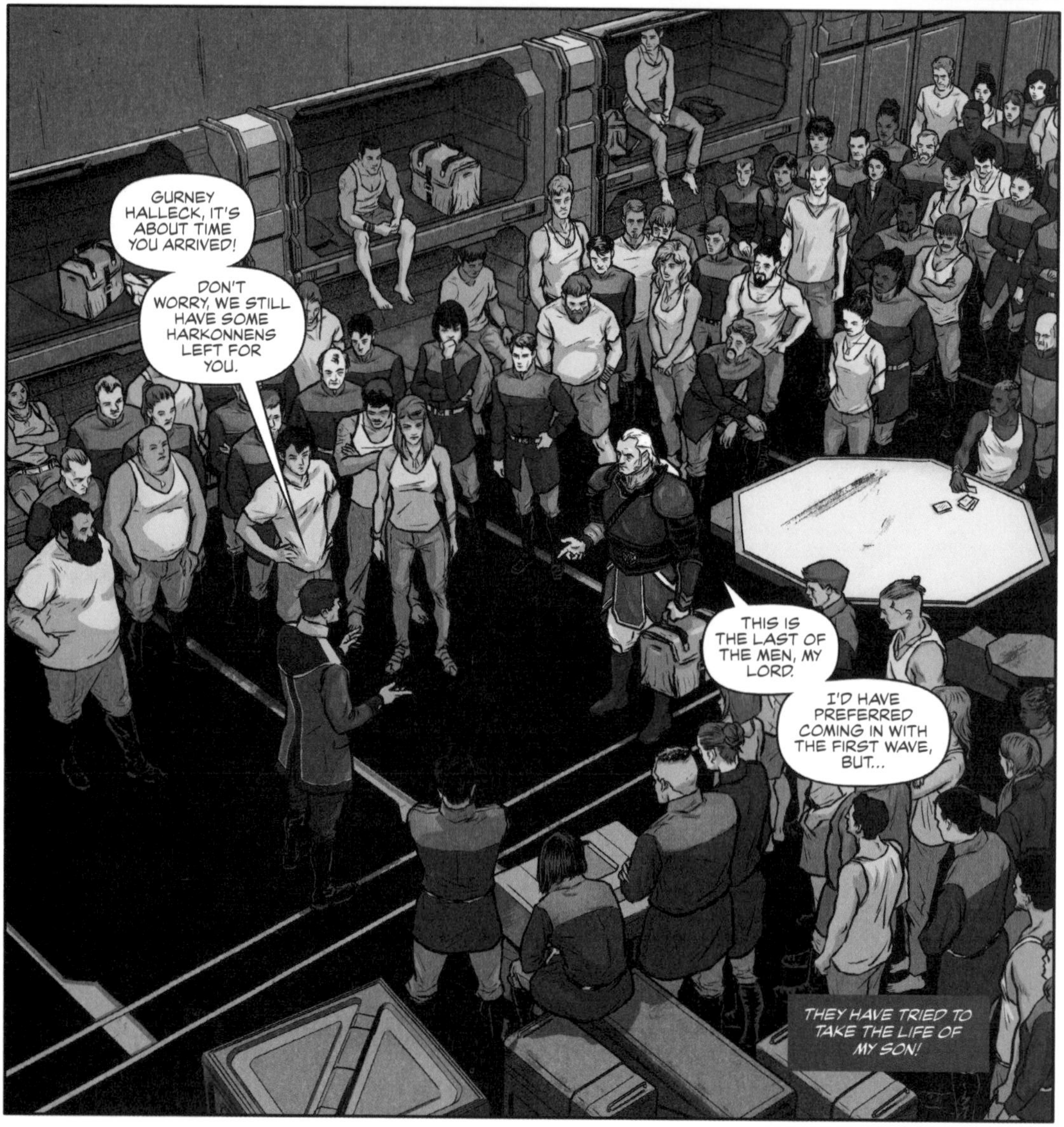
GURNEY HALLECK, IT'S ABOUT TIME YOU ARRIVED!
DON'T WORRY, WE STILL HAVE SOME HARKONNENS LEFT FOR YOU.
THIS IS THE LAST OF THE MEN, MY LORD.
I'D HAVE PREFERRED COMING IN WITH THE FIRST WAVE, BUT...
THEY HAVE TRIED TO TAKE THE LIFE OF MY SON!

STEP ASIDE WITH ME, GURNEY, WHERE WE MAY TALK.

HOW MANY MEN CAN YOU LET HAWAT HAVE? SECURITY HERE IS PROBLEMATIC.

HE WANTS AS MANY MEN AS YOU CAN SPARE—MEN WHO WON'T BALK AT A LITTLE KNIFE WORK.

IN THAT CASE, I CAN LET HIM HAVE THREE HUNDRED OF MY BEST.

AND I HAVE ANOTHER IMPORTANT MISSION FOR YOU, GURNEY. DELAY THAT FRIGATE FOR THE TIME BEING.

WHEN IT LEAVES, A GREAT MANY SPICE WORKERS WILL WANT TO GO.

I WANT YOU TO CONVINCE THEM TO STAY. WE **NEED** THEM.

HOW STRONG A PERSUASION, SIRE?

I WANT THEIR WILLING COOPERATION.

I SUGGEST YOU PLAY A TUNE OR TWO TO SOFTEN THEIR MINDS, THEN TURN ON THE PRESSURE.

"BEHOLD, AS A WILD ASS IN THE DESERT, GO I FORTH TO MY WORK."

THEY HAVE TRIED TO TAKE THE LIFE OF MY SON!

MY FATHER HAS BEEN EXPECTING ME FOR SOME TIME. HE HAS AN IMPORTANT MEETING OUT HERE IN THE COMMAND CENTER.

WE HAD TO BE SURE IT WAS SAFE, SIR.

TWO MOONS...ANOTHER REMINDER OF HOW STRANGE THIS PLACE IS.

I HAVE DREAMED THIS.

O you who know what we suffer here, do not forget us in your prayers.

PAUL...YOU ARE HERE. AND SAFE.

I'M SORRY IT TOOK SO LONG, SIR.

HAWAT TOLD ME THAT HOUSE WAS SECURE! HE IS OLD AND NO LONGER SHARP.

I WAS ANGRY, TOO—AND I BLAMED HAWAT. BUT THE THREAT CAME FROM OUTSIDE THE HOUSE.

AND IT WOULD'VE SUCCEEDED WERE IT NOT FOR THE TRAINING GIVEN ME BY HAWAT.

YOU'RE DEFENDING HIM?

YES. HAWAT WILL PUNISH HIMSELF ENOUGH.

MY LORD, I HAVE JUST LEARNED HOW I FAILED YOU.

IT BECOMES NECESSARY THAT I TENDER MY RESIG—

OH, SIT DOWN AND STOP ACTING THE FOOL.

IF YOU MADE A MISTAKE, IT WAS IN OVERESTIMATING THE HARKONNENS.

AND MY SON HAS BEEN AT GREAT PAINS TO POINT OUT THAT HE CAME THROUGH THIS BECAUSE OF YOUR TRAINING.

THEIR SIMPLE MINDS CAME UP WITH A SIMPLE TRICK.

WE DIDN'T COUNT ON SIMPLE TRICKS.

BUT—

I'LL HEAR NO MORE OF IT. THE INCIDENT IS PAST. WE HAVE MORE PRESSING BUSINESS.

I KNOW WHO MY TRUE FRIENDS ARE, THUFIR. SEND IN THE MEN.

MUCH AFOOT TONIGHT, MY LORD.

THAT IS WHY WE NEED THIS WAR COUNCIL.

THEY ALL KNOW HOW SERIOUS THIS IS. HOW IMPORTANT...

WELL, GENTLEMEN, WE CANNOT EVEN OBEY A SIMPLE ORDER OF THE IMPERIUM WITHOUT THE OLD WAYS CROPPING UP.

THUFIR, WHAT IS YOUR REPORT ON THE FREMEN?

THE FREMEN APPEAR MORE AND MORE TO BE THE ALLIES WE NEED. THEY'RE WAITING TO SEE IF THEY CAN **TRUST** US.

BUT THEY'VE SENT US A GIFT-STILLSUITS OF THEIR OWN MANUFACTURE. IT'S THE ONLY WAY THEY SURVIVE IN THE DEEP DESERT.

YOU LIKE THESE PEOPLE, THUFIR?

DUNCAN IDAHO HAS BEEN AMONG THEM FOR SOME TIME. HE SAYS THEY'RE TO BE ADMIRED.

DO YOU HAVE ANY ESTIMATE ON HOW MANY FREMEN THERE ARE?

THE SIETCH IDAHO VISITED HAD APPROXIMATELY TEN THOUSAND PEOPLE.

AND THERE ARE SAID TO BE MANY SUCH SIETCH COMMUNITIES.

ALL SEEM TO GIVE THEIR ALLEGIANCE TO SOMEONE CALLED LIET. IT MAY BE A PERSON, OR IT MAY BE A LOCAL DEITY.

AND ARE WE CERTAIN THE FREMEN DEAL WITH SMUGGLERS?

THERE ARE MANY SMUGGLERS. IDAHO SAW A SMUGGLER CARAVAN LEAVE THE SIETCH WITH A LARGE LOAD OF SPICE.

GURNEY, I WANT YOU TO CONTACT THE SMUGGLERS, TELL THEM I WILL LEAVE THEIR OPERATIONS ALONE SO LONG AS THEY PAY ME A DUCAL TITHE...WHICH I WILL HOLD IN THE EMPEROR'S NAME.

THUFIR, WERE YOU ABLE TO OBTAIN THE HARKONNEN ACCOUNT BOOKS?

YES, MY LORD. I HAVE SKIMMED THEM AND CAN DO A FIRST APPROXIMATION.

WITH THEIR SPICE OPERATIONS, THE HARKONNENS TOOK TEN BILLION SOLARIS OUT OF HERE EVERY STANDARD YEAR.

IS THERE ANYONE HERE SO NAIVE HE BELIEVES THE HARKONNENS HAVE QUIETLY PACKED UP AND WALKED AWAY FROM ALL THIS MERELY BECAUSE THE EMPEROR ORDERED IT?

THE SPICE OPERATIONS ARE OURS NOW.

WHAT SORT OF EQUIPMENT DID THE HARKONNENS LEAVE BEHIND FOR US?

THE JUDGE OF THE CHANGE CONDUCTED A COMPLETE AUDIT, MY LORD.

WE HAVE A FULL COMPLEMENT OF SANDCRAWLERS, HARVESTERS, SPICE FACTORIES, AND SUPPORTING EQUIPMENT.

THE REPORT, HOWEVER, NEGLECTS TO NOTE THAT LESS THAN HALF OF THEM ARE OPERATIONAL.

AS EXPECTED...

THERE'S NO JUSTICE IN THIS!

JUSTICE? WHO ASKS FOR JUSTICE? WE MAKE OUR OWN JUSTICE. WE MAKE IT HERE ON ARRAKIS—WIN OR DIE.

THUFIR, ARE THERE SANDWORMS BIG ENOUGH TO SWALLOW THAT WHOLE?

THERE'RE WORMS IN THE DEEP DESERT COULD TAKE THIS ENTIRE FACTORY IN ONE GULP.

WHY DON'T WE SHIELD THEM?

SHIELDS ARE DANGEROUS IN THE DESERT, SAID TO DRIVE THE WORMS INTO A FRENZY. THE FREMEN REFUSE TO USE THEM AT ALL. THEY SEEM TO FIND SHIELDS... AMUSING.

WE NEED A SOLID AND PERMANENT PLANETARY BASE HERE. AND THAT MAY DEPEND ON THE FREMEN.

ON CALADAN, WE HAD SEA AND AIR POWER. HERE, WE MUST DEVELOP DESERT POWER.

SORRY I'M LATE, SIRE. I HAVE JUST COME IN FROM THE DESERT.

DUNCAN IDAHO!

GIVE YOUR REPORT. YOU CAN SEE THIS IS ALL TRUSTED STRATEGY STAFF.

WE'VE TAKEN A FORCE OF HARKONNEN MERCENARIES DISGUISED AS FREMEN, AND THE FREMEN SENT A COURIER TO WARN US.

BUT THE HARKONNENS BADLY WOUNDED THE FREMEN MAN.

WE WERE BRINGING HIM HERE FOR TREATMENT WHEN HE DIED.

I TRIED TO HELP HIM, AND I SURPRISED HIM IN AN ATTEMPT TO THROW SOMETHING AWAY...

A KNIFE, M'LORD, A KNIFE THE LIKE OF WHICH YOU'VE NEVER SEEN.

CRYSKNIFE?

KTCH-

KEEP THAT BLADE IN ITS SHEATH!

KLANG

57

LET HIM ENTER, SIRE.

THIS IS STILGAR, CHIEF OF THE SIETCH I VISITED, LEADER OF THOSE WHO WARNED US OF THE HARKONNEN BAND.

WELCOME, SIR. AND WHY SHOULDN'T WE UNSHEATH THIS BLADE?

YOU HAVE EARNED HONOR AMONG US, DUNCAN IDAHO.

I WOULD PERMIT YOU TO SEE THE BLADE OF THE MAN YOU BEFRIENDED.

BUT I DO NOT KNOW THESE OTHERS.

I AM THE DUKE LETO. WOULD YOU PERMIT ME TO SEE THIS BLADE?

I'LL PERMIT YOU TO **EARN** THE RIGHT TO UNSHEATH IT.

WHO'S HE TO TELL US WHAT RIGHTS WE HAVE ON ARRAKIS?

THAT'S THE DUKE HE'S TALKING TO!

ONE MOMENT, PLEASE.

I HONOR AND RESPECT THE PERSONAL DIGNITY OF ANY MAN WHO RESPECTS MY DIGNITY. I AM INDEBTED TO YOU. AND I ALWAYS PAY MY DEBTS.

A CERTAIN RESPONSIBILITY FALLS ON THOSE WHO HAVE SEEN A CRYSKNIFE. THE HARKONNENS HAVE OFFERED A MILLION SOLARIS FOR EVEN ONE SUCH KNIFE.

IF IT IS YOUR CUSTOM THAT THIS KNIFE REMAIN SHEATHED HERE, THEN IT IS SO ORDERED— BY ME.

PTAAHHH!

WHAT THE—

AN INSULT TO THE DUKE!

HOLD!

REMEMBER HOW PRECIOUS WATER IS HERE, SIRE.

THAT WAS A TOKEN OF RESPECT.

PTAAHHH!

WE THANK YOU, STILGAR, FOR THE GIFT OF YOUR BODY'S MOISTURE.

WE ACCEPT IT IN THE SPIRIT WITH WHICH IT IS GIVEN.

YOU MEASURED WELL IN MY SIETCH, DUNCAN IDAHO.

IS THERE A BOND ON YOUR ALLEGIANCE TO YOUR DUKE?

60

HE'S ASKING ME TO ENLIST WITH HIM, SIRE. TO STAY AMONG THE FREMEN.

WOULD HE ACCEPT A DUAL ALLEGIANCE? YOU WOULD SERVE ME, BUT YOU WOULD BE OUR AMBASSADOR AMONG THE FREMEN.

THERE IS PRECEDENT FOR THIS: LIET SERVES TWO MASTERS.

YOUR WATER IS OURS, DUNCAN IDAHO. THE BODY OF OUR FRIEND REMAINS WITH YOUR DUKE.

HIS WATER IS ATREIDES WATER. IT IS A BOND BETWEEN US.

I WILL AWAIT BELOW, WHILE IDAHO MAKES FAREWELL WITH HIS FRIENDS.

THEN HE COMES BACK WITH US TO THE DESERT.

IF THE OTHER FREMEN MATCH HIM, WE'LL SERVE EACH OTHER WELL.

HE IS A FAIR SAMPLE, SIR.

WHY DO THE HARKONNENS WANT SUCH A KNIFE SO BADLY?

A REWARD OF A MILLION SOLARIS?

THE KNIFE IS GROUND FROM A SANDWORM'S TOOTH. IT'S THE MARK OF THE FREMEN, SIRE.

A SPY WHO POSSESSED ONE COULD PENETRATE ANY SIETCH AND CAUSE UNTOLD HARM.

GO AMONG THE FREMEN, DUNCAN.

WE ARE GOING TO HAVE TO MOVE FAST WITH THEM. I'D LIKE FIVE FULL BATTALIONS OF OUR DESERT ARMY.

SOON.

LATER...

THE GUARDS SAID I WOULD FIND YOU HERE.

WHERE IS PAUL, SIRE?

I LEFT HIM IN THE CONFERENCE ROOM. I'M HOPING HE'LL GET SOME REST WITHOUT ME THERE TO DISTRACT HIM.

THUFIR, THE IMPERIAL AND HARKONNEN STOCKPILES OF SPICE ON ARRAKIS ATTRACT MY ATTENTION.

THE EMPEROR HAS MANY, THE HARKONNENS HAVE MORE. AND STOREHOUSES ARE SUSCEPTIBLE TO DESTRUCTION.

IGNORE THE EMPEROR'S HOARD. *DESTROY* WHAT THE HARKONNENS HAVE HIDDEN HERE.

AS YOU SAY, MY LORD. BUT...I HAVE ALREADY FAILED YOU.

THUFIR, SINCE YOU'RE ONE OF THE FEW I CAN TRUST COMPLETELY, THERE'S ANOTHER MATTER BEARS DISCUSSION.

I HAVE CONVINCING REPORTS FROM TWO SOURCES THERE IS A TRAITOR AMONG US.

MY LORD, I DON'T QUITE KNOW HOW TO BROACH THIS.

IT'S A SCRAP OF A NOTE.

KRINKLE

WE TOOK IT FROM A HARKONNEN COURIER.

ACID DESTROYED MUCH OF IT, AND THE COURIER DIED BEFORE WE COULD INTERROGATE HIM.

BUT THE FRAGMENT IS **EXTREMELY** SUGGESTIVE.

Leto will never suspect, and when the blow falls on him from a beloved hand, its source alone should be enough to destroy him.

THE NOTE WAS UNDER THE BARON'S OWN SEAL, AND I'VE AUTHENTICATED IT.

THE LADY JESSICA.

THAT IS WHAT YOU'RE THINKING.

I'D SOONER CUT OFF MY ARMS THAN HURT YOU. BUT WE CANNOT IGNORE IT, MY LORD.

SHE'S BEEN WITH ME FOR SIXTEEN YEARS!

SHE IS THE MOTHER OF MY SON. SHE'S HAD COUNTLESS OPPORTUNITIES...

THE HARKONNENS MEAN TO DESTROY YOU, MY LORD. THEIR INTENT IS NOT JUST TO KILL. THIS COULD BE A WORK OF ART AMONG VENDETTAS.

WHAT BETTER WAY TO DESTROY ME THAN TO SOW SUSPICION OF THE WOMAN I LOVE?

WHAT IF THAT IS THEIR GAME?

FOR NOW, I RECOMMEND CONSTANT SURVEILLANCE, MY LORD. JUST TO BE SURE.

BEFORE YOU GO...THERE'S A FILMCLIP.

YOU ASKED ME ABOUT IT.

WHEN THE ARRAKEEN CROWDS SAW THE YOUNG MASTER, THEY WERE SHOUTING SOMETHING.

I HAVE DETERMINED THAT THE WORD IS "*MAHDI*."

THEY'VE A LEGEND HERE, A PROPHECY, THAT A LEADER WILL COME TO THEM, A CHILD OF A BENE GESSERIT.

IT FOLLOWS THE FAMILIAR MESSIAH PATTERN.

PAUL? RIGHT NOW, I NEED TIME TO THINK.

MESSIAH?

MY LORD.

AT EASE.

THE HARKONNENS HAVE HINDERED AND HOUNDED AND HUNTED ME FOR THE *LAST* TIME!

HERE I MAKE MY STAND! I MUST RULE WITH EYE AND CLAW—AS THE HAWK AMONG LESSER BIRDS.

IT'S A BEAUTIFUL MORNING, SIRE.

YES, IT IS.

"YOU CAN SEE THE DAWN FLOWERS BLOOMING—THINGS HAPPEN FAST HERE IN THE DESERT."

"WHAT ARE THEY DOING THERE?"

"THEY GATHER THE DEW, MY LORD."

"IN THE MOMENTS THEY CAN."

PERHAPS THIS PLANET COULD GROW ON ME.

PERHAPS IT COULD BECOME A GOOD HOME FOR MY SON.

AND IT COULD BE A HIDEOUS PLACE.

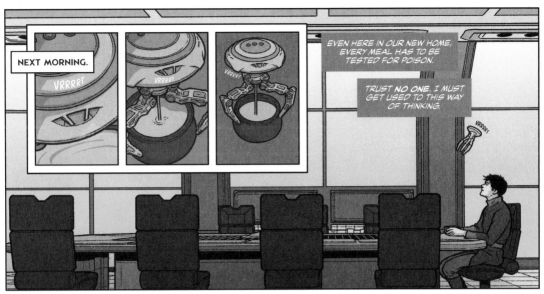

NEXT MORNING.

VRRRRT

VRRRRT

VRRRRT

EVEN HERE IN OUR NEW HOME, EVERY MEAL HAS TO BE TESTED FOR POISON.

TRUST **NO ONE**. I MUST GET USED TO THIS WAY OF THINKING.

VRRRRT

WHY DO THEY CALL ME THAT...?

MAHDI! MAHDI! LISAN AL-GAIB!

PAUL, I NEED TO SPEAK WITH YOU PRIVATELY. I'M DOING A HATEFUL THING, BUT I MUST.

A HATEFUL THING.

WHAT DO YOU MEAN, SIR?

BECAUSE THE HARKONNENS THINK TO TRICK ME BY MAKING ME DISTRUST YOUR MOTHER.

I HAVE A SCRAP OF A NOTE THAT IMPLIES SHE MEANS TO BETRAY US. THEY DON'T KNOW THAT I'D SOONER DISTRUST MYSELF.

YOU MIGHT JUST AS WELL MISTRUST ME.

THEY HAVE TO THINK THEY'VE SUCCEEDED. THEY MUST THINK ME THIS MUCH OF A FOOL.

IT MUST LOOK REAL. EVEN YOUR MOTHER MAY NOT KNOW THE SHAM.

BUT, SIR! WHY?

YOUR MOTHER'S RESPONSE MUST **NOT** BE AN ACT. TOO MUCH RIDES ON THIS. I HOPE TO SMOKE OUT A TRAITOR.

SHE MUST BE HURT THIS WAY SO THAT SHE DOES NOT SUFFER GREATER HURT.

WHY DO YOU TELL ME, FATHER? MAYBE I'LL GIVE IT AWAY.

THEY'LL NOT WATCH YOU IN THIS THING. YOU'LL KEEP THE SECRET. YOU MUST.

THIS WAY, IF ANYTHING SHOULD HAPPEN TO ME, YOU CAN TELL HER THE TRUTH—THAT I NEVER DOUBTED HER, NOT FOR THE SMALLEST INSTANT. I SHOULD WANT HER TO KNOW THIS.

NOTHING'S GOING TO HAPPEN TO YOU, SIR. THE—

BE SILENT, SON.

I SHOULD WED YOUR MOTHER, MAKE HER MY DUCHESS. ONLY BECAUSE OF POLITICS DO I LEAVE MYSELF AVAILABLE FOR THE DAUGHTERS OF OTHER NOBLES.

I AM TIRED OF IT. I SHOULD MARRY HER...

I HAVE TO HAVE SOMEONE I CAN SAY THESE THINGS TO, SON. THIS IS YOUR INHERITANCE, PAUL.

WHAT IS TO BECOME OF YOU IF ANYTHING HAPPENS TO ME?

WE HAVE SOMETHING SPECIAL TODAY.

THE IMPERIAL PLANETOLOGIST AND JUDGE OF THE CHANGE, A MAN NAMED **KYNES**, WILL TAKE US OUT TO THE DEEP DESERT SO WE CAN OBSERVE SPICE OPERATIONS.

I WANT YOU TO GO WITH ME.

YES!

ARRAKEEN SPACEPORT.

IS THIS REALLY THE PROPHECY? THE BOY FITS IT SO WELL.

KYNES. IMPERIAL PLANETARY ECOLOGIST AND JUDGE OF THE CHANGE.

THAT GUARD IS USING A SHIELD! ARRAKIS HAS A SURPRISE FOR THEM THERE!

STAY HERE. I WILL GO SEE THIS DUKE.

THE EMPEROR HAS ORDERED ME TO BETRAY THESE PEOPLE...

BUT WE ARE FAR FROM THE IMPERIUM.

THE DUKE...HE WEARS THE STILLSUIT WE GAVE HIM, BUT IT IS AWKWARD FOR HIM.

KYNES. WE'VE BEEN WAITING FOR YOU.

THE BOY PAUL, THOUGH...

THE MAHDI WILL BE AWARE OF THINGS OTHERS CANNOT SEE.

I'VE BRIEFED THIS MAN ON PROPER BEHAVIOR IN YOUR PRESENCE, MY LORD.

HE HAS.

70

YOU'RE THE ECOLOGIST.

MY LORD DUKE. WE PREFER THE OLD TITLE HERE. PLANETOLOGIST.

SON, THIS IS THE JUDGE OF THE CHANGE, THE MAN SENT HERE TO SEE THAT THE FORMS ARE OBEYED IN OUR ASSUMPTION OF POWER OVER THIS FIEF. AND THIS IS MY SON.

ARE YOU A FREMEN?

I AM ACCEPTED IN BOTH SIETCH AND VILLAGE, YOUNG MASTER. BUT I AM IN HIS MAJESTY'S SERVICE.

DR. KYNES, I UNDERSTAND WE HAVE YOU TO THANK FOR OUR STILLSUITS AND THESE CLOAKS.

I HOPE THEY FIT WELL, MY LORD. THEY'RE OF FREMEN MAKE. THE BEST ON ARRAKIS. THEY MAY SAVE YOUR LIFE.

WE WON'T NEED THEM TODAY. WE CAN CARRY PLENTY OF WATER.

WE DON'T INTEND TO BE OUT LONG, AND WE'LL HAVE AIR COVER. IT ISN'T LIKELY WE'D BE FORCED DOWN.

YOU NEVER TALK OF LIKELIHOODS ON ARRAKIS. YOU SPEAK ONLY OF POSSIBILITIES.

THE DUKE IS TO BE ADDRESSED AS MY LORD OR SIRE!

NOW, GURNEY. OUR WAYS ARE NEW HERE. WE MUST MAKE ALLOWANCES.

71

WE ARE INDEBTED TO YOU, DR. KYNES. THESE SUITS AND YOUR CONSIDERATION FOR OUR WELFARE WILL BE REMEMBERED.

THE O.C. BIBLE SAYS "THE GIFT IS THE BLESSING OF THE GIVER."

LISAN AL-GAIB!

MUR MUR

LISAN AL-GAIB!

ENOUGH!

MOST OF THE DESERT NATIVES HERE ARE A SUPERSTITIOUS LOT. PAY NO ATTENTION TO THEM. THEY MEAN NO HARM.

THE PROPHECY AGAIN...

SHOULDN'T WE BE GOING, SIRE?

I'LL FLY MY OWN 'THOPTER. KYNES CAN SIT UP FRONT WITH ME TO DIRECT ME.

GURNEY, YOU AND PAUL TAKE THE REAR SEATS.

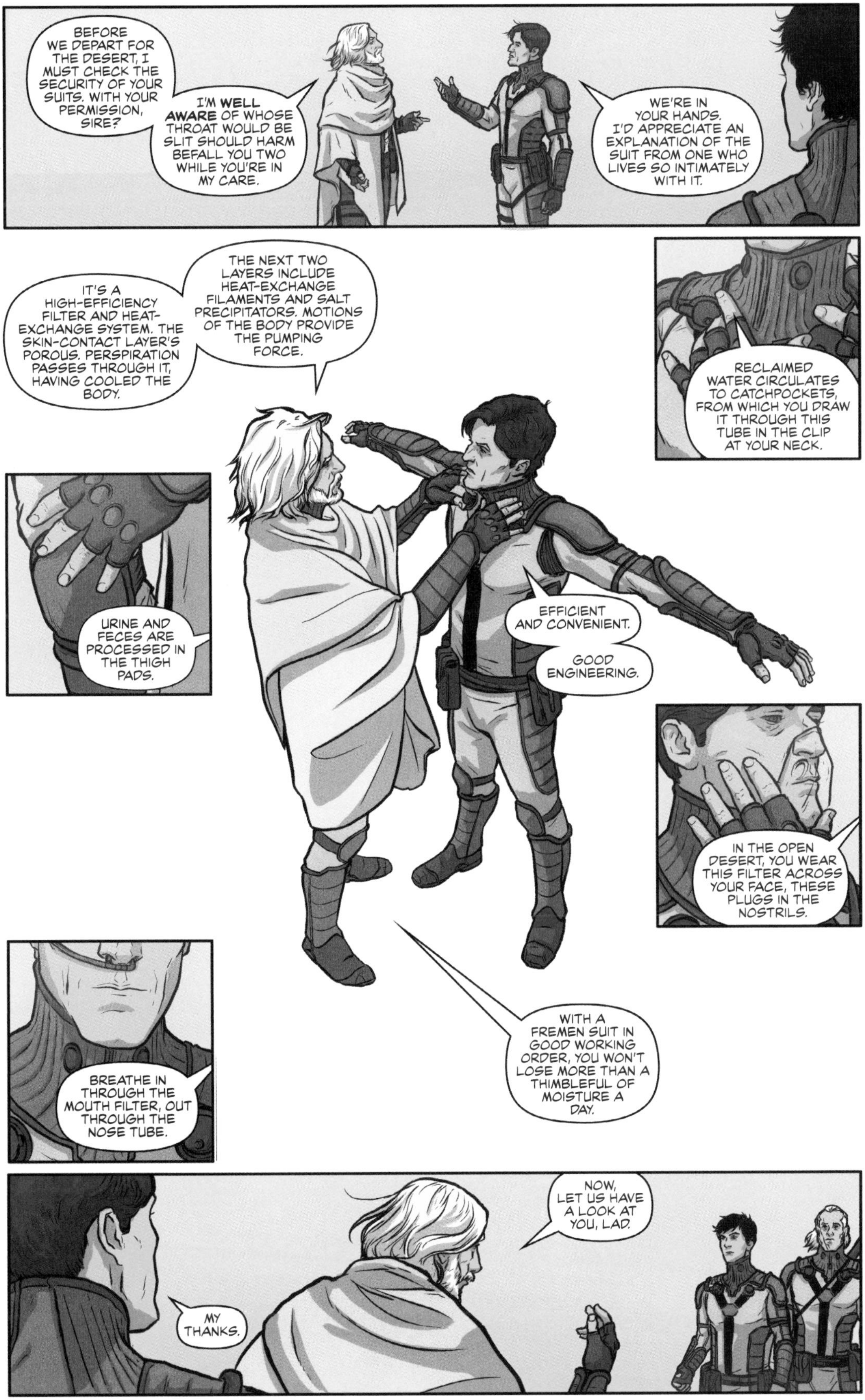
BEFORE WE DEPART FOR THE DESERT, I MUST CHECK THE SECURITY OF YOUR SUITS. WITH YOUR PERMISSION, SIRE?
I'M **WELL AWARE** OF WHOSE THROAT WOULD BE SLIT SHOULD HARM BEFALL YOU TWO WHILE YOU'RE IN MY CARE.
WE'RE IN YOUR HANDS. I'D APPRECIATE AN EXPLANATION OF THE SUIT FROM ONE WHO LIVES SO INTIMATELY WITH IT.
IT'S A HIGH-EFFICIENCY FILTER AND HEAT-EXCHANGE SYSTEM. THE SKIN-CONTACT LAYER'S POROUS. PERSPIRATION PASSES THROUGH IT, HAVING COOLED THE BODY.
THE NEXT TWO LAYERS INCLUDE HEAT-EXCHANGE FILAMENTS AND SALT PRECIPITATORS. MOTIONS OF THE BODY PROVIDE THE PUMPING FORCE.
RECLAIMED WATER CIRCULATES TO CATCHPOCKETS, FROM WHICH YOU DRAW IT THROUGH THIS TUBE IN THE CLIP AT YOUR NECK.
URINE AND FECES ARE PROCESSED IN THE THIGH PADS.
EFFICIENT AND CONVENIENT.
GOOD ENGINEERING.
IN THE OPEN DESERT, YOU WEAR THIS FILTER ACROSS YOUR FACE, THESE PLUGS IN THE NOSTRILS.
BREATHE IN THROUGH THE MOUTH FILTER, OUT THROUGH THE NOSE TUBE.
WITH A FREMEN SUIT IN GOOD WORKING ORDER, YOU WON'T LOSE MORE THAN A THIMBLEFUL OF MOISTURE A DAY.
NOW, LET US HAVE A LOOK AT YOU, LAD.
MY THANKS.

YOU'VE WORN A STILLSUIT BEFORE? DID SOMEONE ADJUST IT FOR YOU?

NO. THIS IS THE FIRST TIME.

YOUR DESERT BOOTS ARE FITTED SLIP-FASHION AT THE ANKLES.

WHO TOLD YOU TO DO THAT?

IT... SEEMED THE RIGHT WAY.

THAT IT MOST CERTAINLY IS.

"HE SHALL KNOW YOUR WAYS AS THOUGH BORN TO THEM."

YOU'LL HEAD SOUTHEAST OVER THE SHIELD WALL.

THAT'S WHERE I TOLD YOUR SANDMASTER TO CONCENTRATE HIS EQUIPMENT.

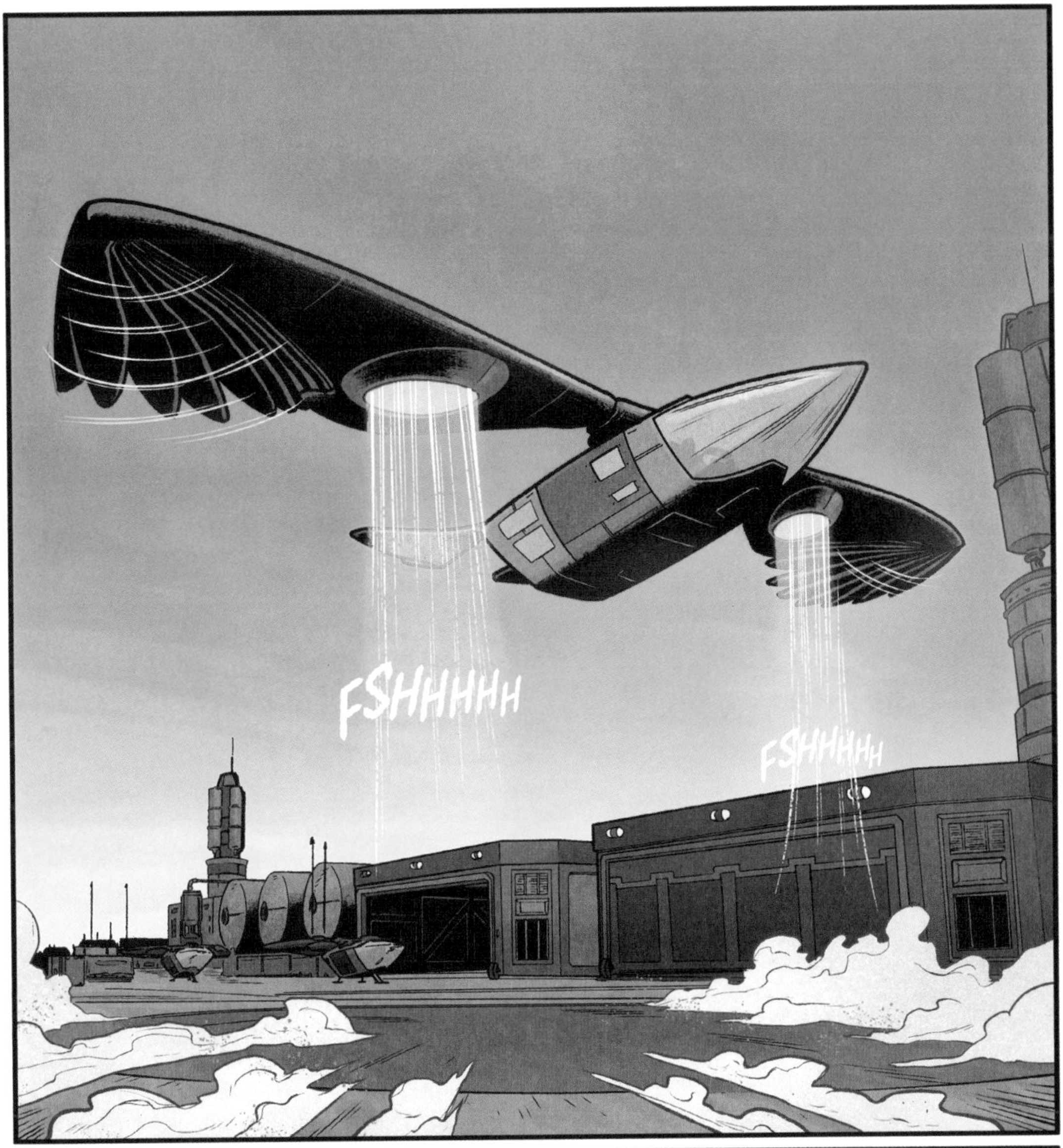
FSHHHHH
FSHHHHH

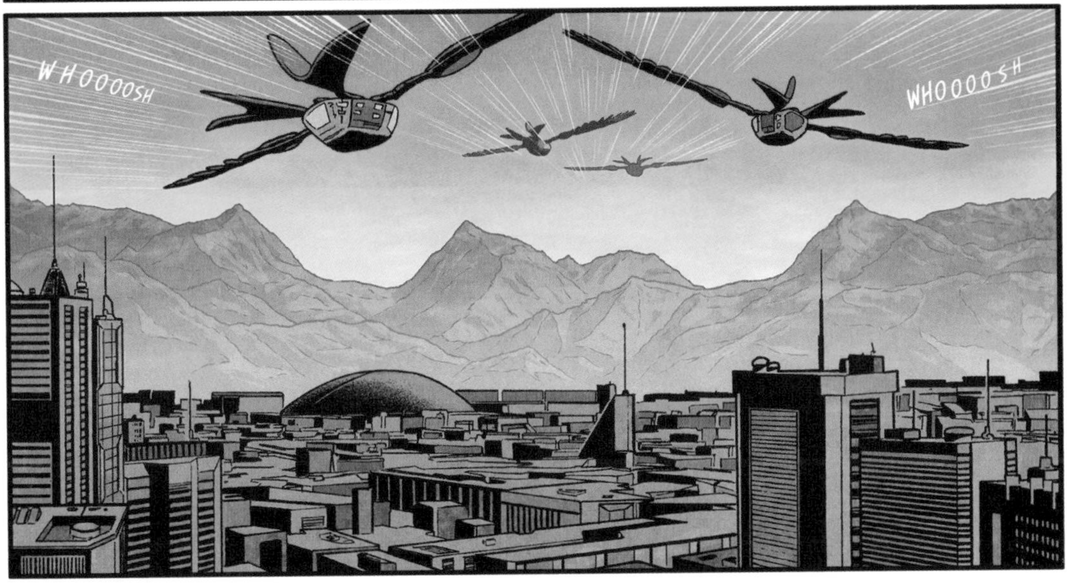
WHOOOOSH
WHOOOOSH

WHEN YOU REPORT TO THE EMPEROR ON THE CHANGE OF GOVERNMENT HERE, KYNES, WILL YOU SAY WE OBSERVED THE RULES?

THE HARKONNENS LEFT, MY LORD. YOU CAME. WHAT ELSE IS THERE TO SAY?

I AM THE JUDGE OF THE CHANGE, BUT I AM PRIMARILY THE IMPERIAL PLANETOLOGIST.

AND WHAT, EXACTLY ARE YOUR DUTIES?

IT IS MOSTLY DRY LAND BIOLOGY AND BOTANY... SOME GEOLOGICAL WORK—CORE DRILLING AND TESTING.

YOU NEVER REALLY EXHAUST THE POSSIBILITIES OF AN ENTIRE PLANET.

DO YOU ALSO INVESTIGATE THE SPICE?

A CURIOUS QUESTION...

THE HARKONNENS DISCOURAGED INVESTIGATION OF THE SPICE.

BUT WE ARE NOT HARKONNENS. I DON'T CARE IF YOU STUDY THE SPICE AS LONG AS I SHARE WHAT YOU DISCOVER.

COME AROUND TWO DEGREES MORE SOUTHERLY, MY LORD. THERE'S A BLOW COMING UP FROM THE WEST. WE'LL WANT TO SKIRT THE EDGE.

THE DUST CAN CLOG INTAKES, DECREASE VISIBILITY.

WILL WE SEE ACTUAL SPICE MINING TODAY?

HAS ANYONE EVER WALKED OUT OF THE DESERT?

NOT FROM THE DEEP DESERT. MEN HAVE WALKED OUT OF THE SECOND ZONE SEVERAL TIMES.

THEY'VE SURVIVED BY CROSSING THE ROCK AREAS WHERE WORMS SELDOM GO.

AH-H, THE WORMS. I MUST SEE ONE SOMETIME.

YOU MAY SEE ONE TODAY.

WHEREVER THERE IS SPICE, THERE ARE WORMS.

IS THERE RELATIONSHIP BETWEEN WORM AND SPICE?

THEY DEFEND SPICE SANDS. EACH WORM HAS A TERRITORY.

AS TO THE SPICE...WHO KNOWS?

DUST CLOUD AHEAD, SIRE.

I SEE IT, GURNEY.

THAT'S WHAT WE SEEK. ONE OF YOUR FACTORY CRAWLERS.

THE CLOUD IS EXPELLED SAND AFTER THE SPICE HAS BEEN EXTRACTED.

AIRCRAFT OVERHEAD. I SEE TWO...FOUR SPOTTERS. THEY'RE WATCHING FOR WORMSIGN.

THE WORM ALWAYS COMES, EH?

ALWAYS.

"THE SPOTTERS WILL REPORT WORMSIGN, TO GIVE WARNING TO THE CREW."

"THERE SHOULD BE A CARRYALL SOMEWHERE."

"THE CARRYALL WILL RESCUE THE CRAWLER, THE CREW, AND THE LOAD OF SPICE BEFORE THE WORM ARRIVES."

CHUG-CHUG CHUG-CHUG CHUG-CHUG

WE'LL KEEP WATCH AS WELL, KYNES. WE'VE ALREADY LOST TOO MUCH EQUIPMENT.

IS THAT WORMSIGN? THERE?

"WORM. BIG ONE."

CALLING CRAWLER AT DELTA AJAX NINER. WORMSIGN WARNING. ACKNOWLEDGE.

WHO CALLS DELTA AJAX NINER? OVER.

UNLISTED FLIGHT—NORTH OF YOU ABOUT THREE KILOMETERS.

WORMSIGN IS ON INTERCEPT COURSE. ESTIMATED CONTACT TWENTY-FIVE MINUTES.

THIS IS SPOTTER CONTROL.

SIGHTING CONFIRMED. STAND BY FOR CONTACT FIX.

THEY SEEM PRETTY CALM ABOUT IT.

CONTACT IN TWENTY-SIX MINUTES MINUS. THAT WAS A SHARP ESTIMATE.

WHO'S ON THAT UNLISTED FLIGHT? OVER.

SPOTTER CREDIT TO THE DUKE LETO ATREIDES. OVER.

NOW TELL THEM IT'S THE DUKE'S WISH THAT THEY DIVIDE THE SPOTTER BONUS AMONGST THEMSELVES.

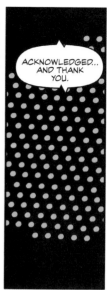

ACKNOWLEDGED... AND THANK YOU.

THIS LETS THE MEN KNOW THEIR DUKE IS CONCERNED FOR THEIR SAFETY. WORD WILL GET AROUND.

SHWISH

GURNEY IS ALSO VERY TALENTED IN PUBLIC RELATIONS.

WHAT HAPPENS NOW?

THERE'S A CARRYALL WING SOMEWHERE CLOSE. IT'LL COME IN AND LIFT OFF THE CRAWLER.

GET IN CLOSE, MY LORD. YOU'LL FIND THIS INTERESTING.

"RICH SPICE BED BY THE COLOR."

CHUG-C
CHUG-CHUG
CHUG-CHUG
CHUG-CH
UG-CHUG

"THEY'LL CONTINUE WORKING UNTIL THE LAST MINUTE."

SHOULDN'T WE BE HEARING THEM CALL IN THE CARRYALL?

ANY OF YOU SEE THE WING? HE ISN'T ANSWERING.

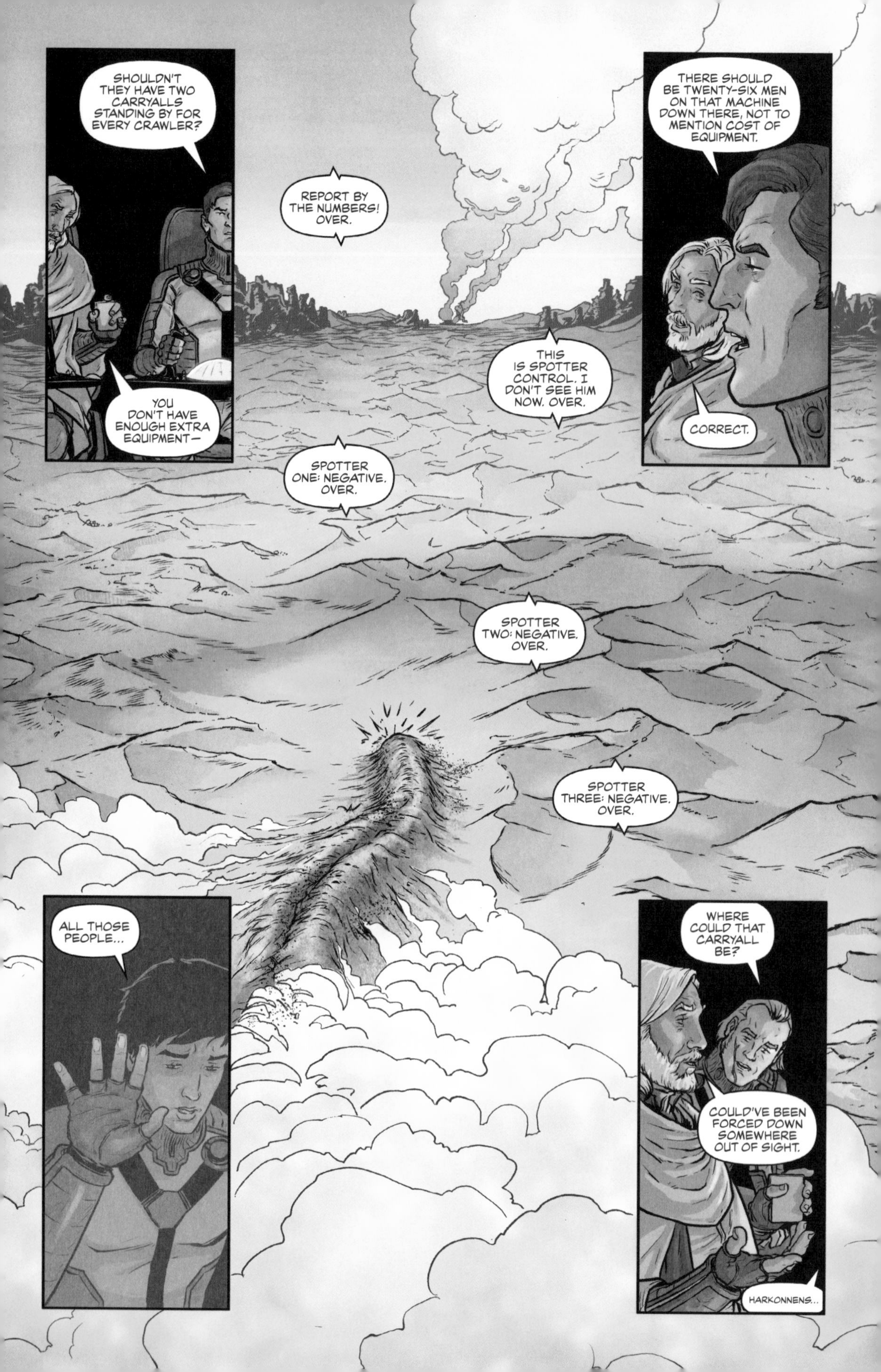
SHOULDN'T THEY HAVE TWO CARRYALLS STANDING BY FOR EVERY CRAWLER?
YOU DON'T HAVE ENOUGH EXTRA EQUIPMENT—
REPORT BY THE NUMBERS! OVER.
THERE SHOULD BE TWENTY-SIX MEN ON THAT MACHINE DOWN THERE, NOT TO MENTION COST OF EQUIPMENT.
CORRECT.
THIS IS SPOTTER CONTROL. I DON'T SEE HIM NOW. OVER.
SPOTTER ONE: NEGATIVE. OVER.
SPOTTER TWO: NEGATIVE. OVER.
SPOTTER THREE: NEGATIVE. OVER.
ALL THOSE PEOPLE...
WHERE COULD THAT CARRYALL BE?
COULD'VE BEEN FORCED DOWN SOMEWHERE OUT OF SIGHT.
HARKONNENS...

THIS IS YOUR DUKE. WE ARE COMING DOWN TO TAKE OFF DELTA AJAX NINER'S CREW. ALL SPOTTERS ARE ORDERED TO COMPLY.

...ALMOST A FULL LOAD OF SPICE! WE CAN'T LEAVE THAT FOR A DAMNED WORM!

DAMN THE SPICE! WE CAN ALWAYS GET MORE SPICE.

THERE ARE SEATS IN OUR SHIPS FOR ALL BUT THREE OF YOU.

DRAW STRAWS OR DECIDE ANY WAY YOU LIKE WHO'S TO GO. BUT YOU'RE GOING, AND THAT'S AN ORDER!

HOW MUCH TIME?

NINE MINUTES.

THIS SHIP HAS MORE POWER THAN THE OTHERS. IF WE TOOK OFF UNDER JET WITH THREE-QUARTER WINGS, WE COULD CROWD IN AN ADDITIONAL MAN.

WITH FOUR EXTRA MEN ABOARD ON A JET TAKEOFF, WE COULD SNAP THE WINGS, SIRE.

FSHHHHH

FSHHHHH

NOT ON THIS SHIP.

CHUG-CHUG

CHUG-CHUG

CHUG-CHUG

CHUG-CHU

THAT SMELL... STRONG CINNAMON!

SPICE.

GURNEY, YOU AND PAUL TOSS OUT THAT REAR SEAT.

WHY THE DEVIL AREN'T THEY COMING OUT OF THAT MACHINE?

THEY'RE HOPING THE CARRYALL WILL SHOW UP. THEY STILL HAVE A FEW MINUTES.

COME ON!!!

ESCORT SHIPS—TWO OF YOU TOSS OUT YOUR SHIELD GENERATORS.

YOU CAN CARRY ONE MORE THAT WAY. WE'RE NOT LEAVING ANY MEN FOR THAT MONSTER.

ALL RIGHT, YOU IN DELTA AJAX NINER! OUT! NOW! THIS IS A COMMAND FROM YOUR DUKE!

ON THE DOUBLE OR I'LL CUT THAT CRAWLER APART WITH A LASGUN!

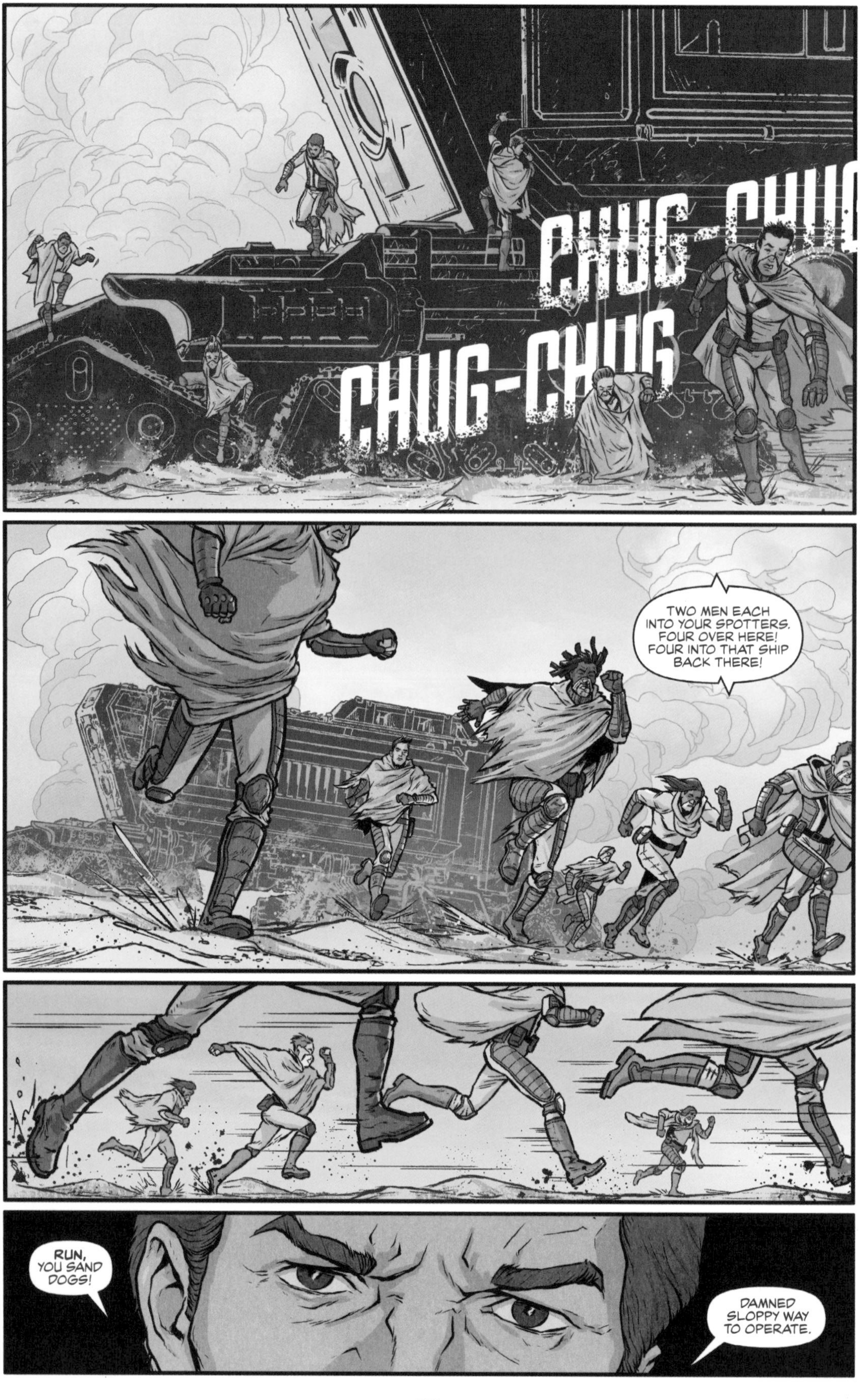
CHUG-CHUG
CHUG-CHUG
TWO MEN EACH INTO YOUR SPOTTERS. FOUR OVER HERE! FOUR INTO THAT SHIP BACK THERE!
RUN, YOU SAND DOGS!
DAMNED SLOPPY WAY TO OPERATE.

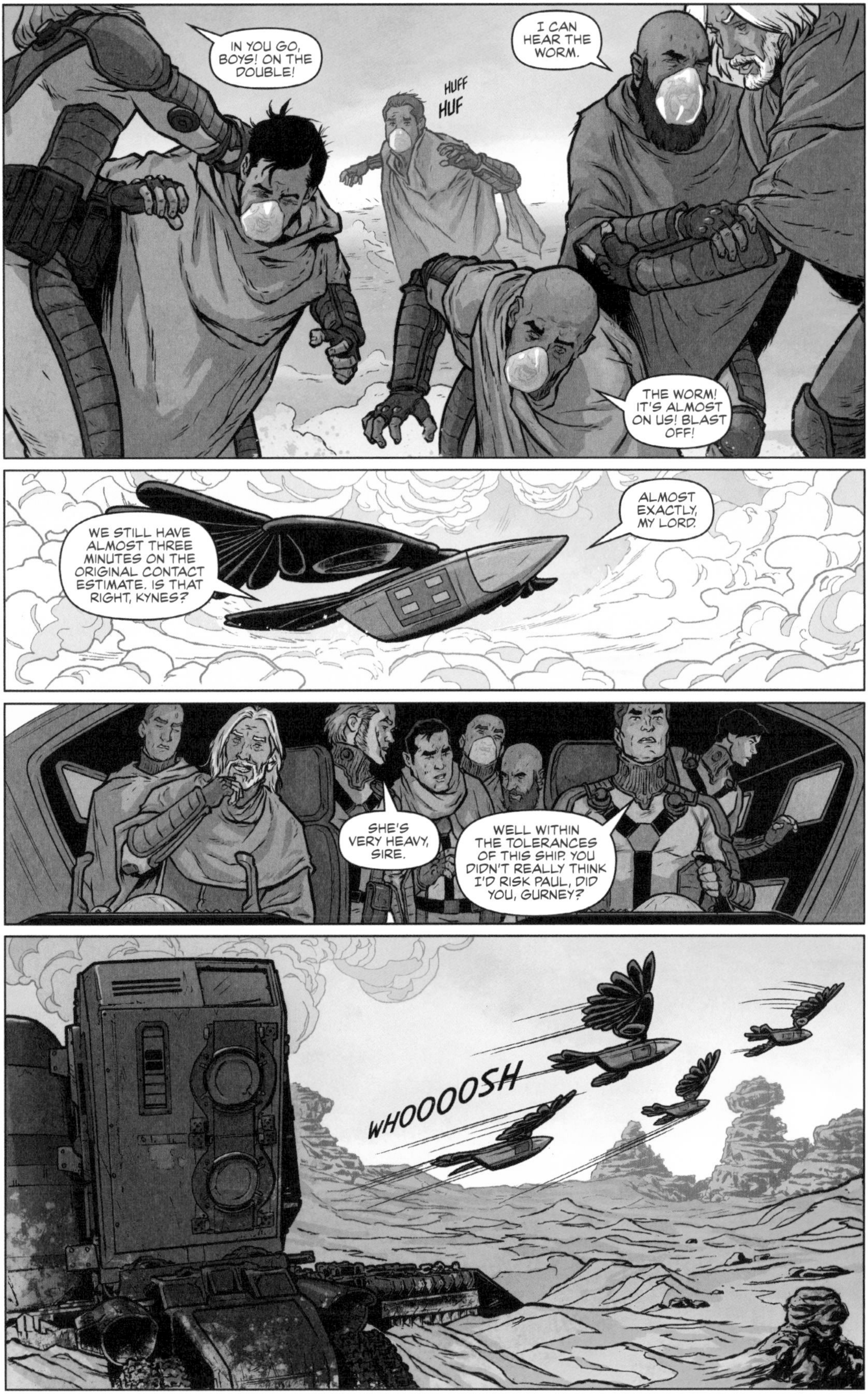
IN YOU GO, BOYS! ON THE DOUBLE!
HUFF HUF
I CAN HEAR THE WORM.
THE WORM! IT'S ALMOST ON US! BLAST OFF!
WE STILL HAVE ALMOST THREE MINUTES ON THE ORIGINAL CONTACT ESTIMATE. IS THAT RIGHT, KYNES?
ALMOST EXACTLY, MY LORD.
SHE'S VERY HEAVY, SIRE.
WELL WITHIN THE TOLERANCES OF THIS SHIP. YOU DIDN'T REALLY THINK I'D RISK PAUL, DID YOU, GURNEY?
WHOOOOSH

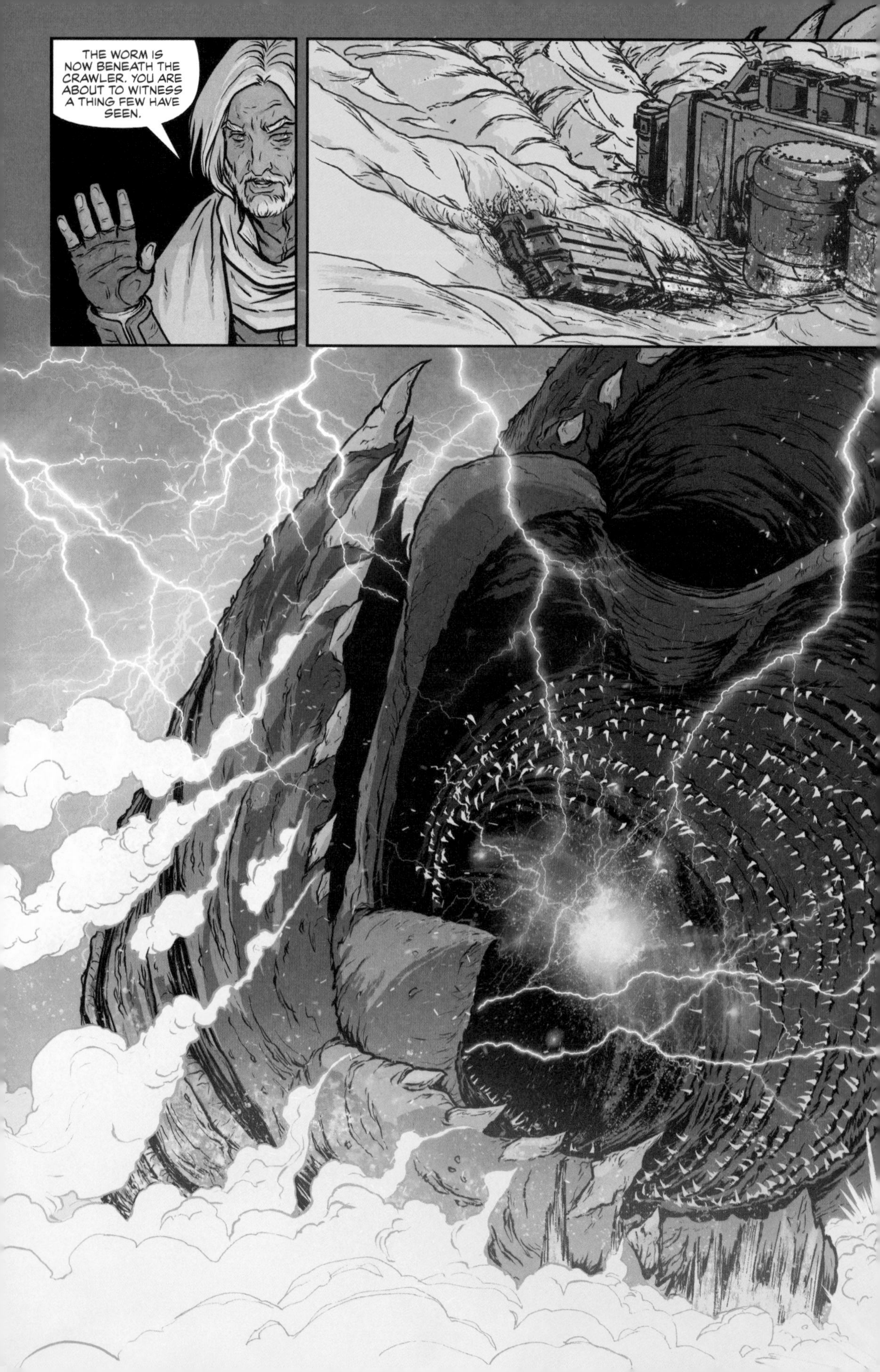
THE WORM IS NOW BENEATH THE CRAWLER. YOU ARE ABOUT TO WITNESS A THING FEW HAVE SEEN.

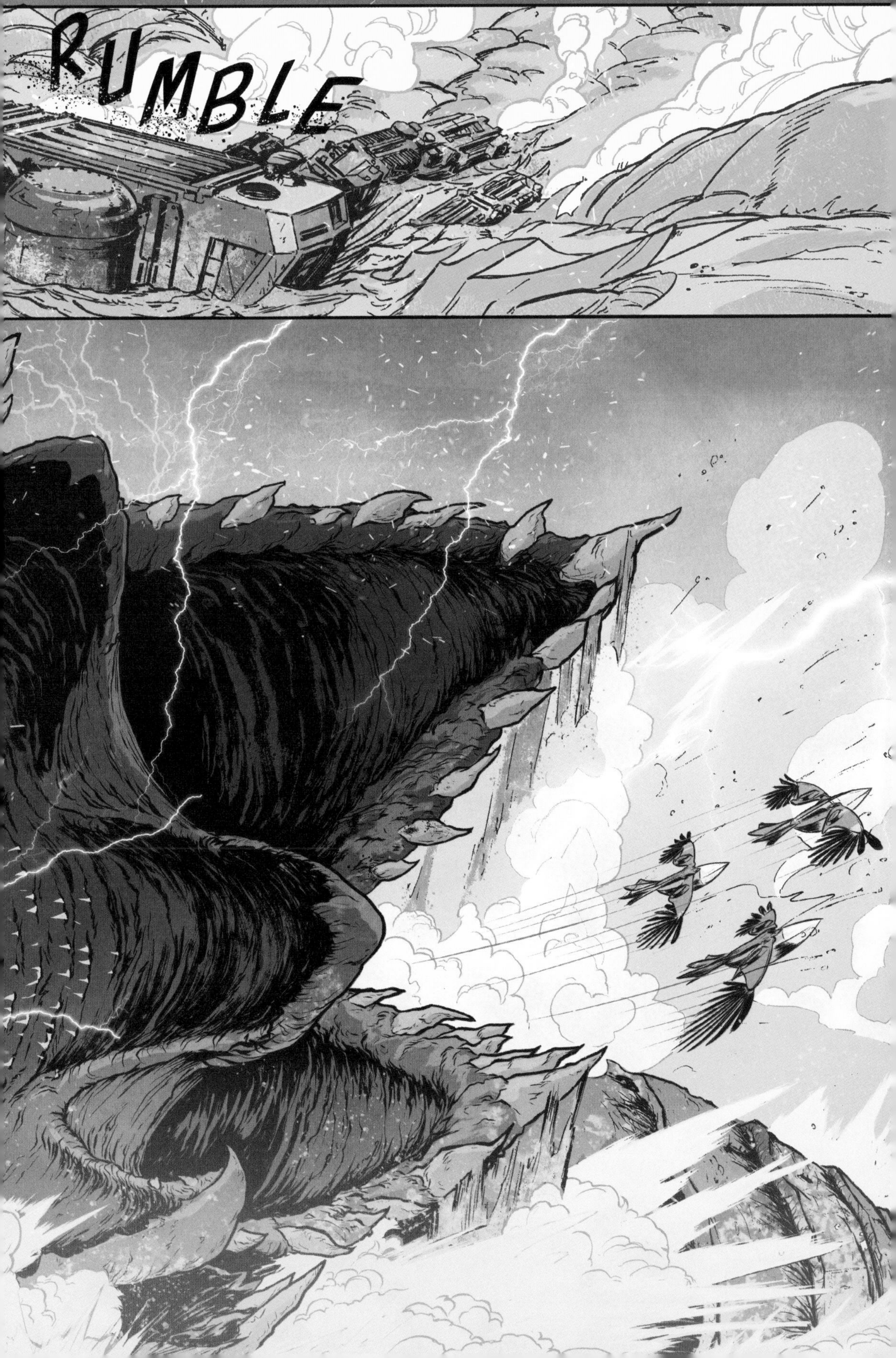
RUMBLE

SOMEONE IS GOING TO PAY FOR THIS. I **PROMISE** YOU THAT.

CURSE THIS HELLHOLE!

THIS IS CRIMINAL WASTE!

GOT ALL OUR FLOGGIN' SPICE!

"GONE...ALL GONE."

BLESS THE MAKER AND HIS WATER. BLESS THE COMING AND GOING OF HIM.

MAY HIS PASSAGE CLEANSE THE WORLD.

MAY HE KEEP THE WORLD FOR HIS PEOPLE.

WHAT'S THAT YOU'RE SAYING?

WHO'S THAT DOWN THERE?

"TWO FREMEN CAME ALONG FOR THE RIDE, SIR. THEY KNEW THE RISKS."

YOU WASTE FUEL HERE, SIRE.

WHY WASN'T ANYTHING SAID ABOUT THEM? HOW DID THEY ESCAPE?

"WHEN GOD HATH ORDAINED A CREATURE TO DIE IN A PARTICULAR PLACE, HE CAUSETH THAT CREATURE'S WANTS TO DIRECT HIM TO THAT PLACE."

THIS DUKE WAS CONCERNED MORE OVER THE MEN THAN HE WAS OVER THE SPICE. HE RISKED *HIS OWN* LIFE AND THAT OF *HIS SON* TO SAVE THE MEN.

HE PASSED OFF THE LOSS OF A SPICE CRAWLER WITH A GESTURE. THE THREAT TO MEN'S LIVES HAD HIM IN A RAGE.

A LEADER SUCH AS THAT WOULD COMMAND FANATIC LOYALTY. HE WOULD BE DIFFICULT TO DEFEAT.

I LIKE THIS DUKE...

ARRAKEEN RESIDENCY.

THE NIGHT OF DUKE LETO ATREIDES' FIRST FORMAL BANQUET.

A FINE BANQUET FOR THE MOST IMPORTANT, CURIOUS, TREACHEROUS PEOPLE ON ARRAKIS. ENEMIES, POSSIBLY...OR ALLIES.

BUT EVEN AT A BANQUET LIKE THIS, WE MUST USE POISON SNOOPERS TO REASSURE THE GUESTS. WHAT DOES THAT SAY ABOUT OUR SOCIETY?

A FLAGON OF WATER FOR EACH GUEST, BECAUSE I AM REQUIRED TO SHOW LARGESSE...BUT IN THIS PLACE, SUCH AN AMOUNT OF WATER WOULD KEEP A POOR ARRAKEEN FAMILY FOR A YEAR.

MAPES, WHAT ARE YOU DOING THERE?

THESE ARE LAVING BASINS, MY LORD.

IT IS THE CUSTOM FOR GUESTS TO DIP THEIR HANDS IN THE WATER, SPLASH SOME ON THE FLOOR, AND DRY THEIR HANDS ON THE TOWELS.

THEY SLOP MANY CUPS OF WATER, AND THE SODDEN TOWELS PILE UP.

AFTER THE DINNER, BEGGARS GATHER OUTSIDE THE RESIDENCY, WHERE THEY ARE OFFERED THE WATER SQUEEZINGS FROM THE TOWELS...

JUST A FEW DROPS OF WATER.

EVERY DEGRADATION OF THE SPIRIT THAT CAN BE CONCEIVED.

THE CUSTOM STOPS HERE!

YOU THERE! HAVE THESE BASINS AND TOWELS REMOVED.

BUT... NOBLE BORN...

I KNOW THE CUSTOM! TAKE THESE BASINS TO THE FRONT DOOR.

WHILE WE'RE EATING AND UNTIL WE'VE FINISHED, EACH BEGGAR WHO CALLS MAY HAVE A FULL CUP OF WATER. UNDERSTOOD?

BUT...

I SEE NOW! SHE IS THE ONE WHO SELLS SQUEEZINGS TO THE POOR WRETCHES.

I'M POSTING A GUARD TO SEE THAT MY ORDERS ARE CARRIED OUT TO THE LETTER.

NOW HURRY, WE ARE ALMOST READY FOR THE BANQUET.

I SEE JESSICA IS MANAGING THE GUESTS QUITE WELL...

THE PLANETOLOGIST, A GUILD BANKER, A WATER-SHIPPER. WHAT DO THEY REALLY WANT?

EVEN IF SHE WASN'T THE HOSTESS, MY JESSICA WOULD DOMINATE THE GROUP...

AND DUNCAN IDAHO...HAWAT HAS GIVEN HIM ORDERS. UNDER THE PRETEXT OF GUARDING JESSICA, HE WILL KEEP HER UNDER CONSTANT SURVEILLANCE.

AND PAUL...WHAT A CATCH A DUCAL HEIR WOULD MAKE AS A FUTURE HUSBAND. HE WILL WEAR THE TITLE WELL ONCE I AM GONE...

HE DID NOT WANT TO ATTEND THIS BANQUET, BUT I TOLD HIM HE HAD A POSITION TO UPHOLD. HE IS ALMOST A MAN.

IS IT TRUE THE DUKE WILL PUT IN WEATHER CONTROL?

WE HAVEN'T GONE THAT FAR IN OUR THINKING, SIR.

APOLOGIES FOR MY LATE ARRIVAL. A THING NEEDED DOING.

I ONLY JUST LEARNED OF A CUSTOM THAT DIRTY WATER AND DAMP TOWELS FROM GUESTS WASHING THEIR HANDS WERE BEING SOLD TO THE POOR OUT IN THE STREETS.

I PUT AN END TO THAT PRACTICE.

DOES THE DUKE IMPLY **CRITICISM** OF OUR CUSTOM?

THE CUSTOM HAS BEEN CHANGED.

AND WHAT ABOUT THE CONSERVATORY YOU KEEP IN THIS RESIDENCY? AN APPALLING WASTE OF WATER.

DO YOU INTEND TO CONTINUE FLAUNTING IT IN PEOPLE'S FACES... MY LORD?

WE INTEND TO KEEP THE CONSERVATORY, CERTAINLY, BUT ONLY TO HOLD IT IN TRUST FOR THE PEOPLE OF ARRAKIS.

IT IS OUR DREAM THAT SOMEDAY THE CLIMATE OF ARRAKIS MAY BE CHANGED SUFFICIENTLY TO GROW SUCH PLANTS ANYWHERE IN THE OPEN.

WATER CUSTOMS ARE **POWER** HERE ON ARRAKIS.

"AND THEY SHALL SHARE YOUR PRECIOUS DREAM..."

AH, DR. KYNES. YOU'VE COME IN FROM TRAMPING AROUND WITH YOUR MOBS OF FREMEN. HOW GRACIOUS OF YOU.

DINNER IS SERVED!

THE CUSTOM HERE IS FOR HOST AND HOSTESS TO FOLLOW THEIR GUESTS TO TABLE.

SHALL WE CHANGE THAT ONE, TOO, MY LORD?

THAT SEEMS A GOODLY CUSTOM.

WE SHALL LET IT STAND FOR NOW.

I MUST SPEAK COLDLY TO HER.

THE ILLUSION THAT I SUSPECT HER OF TREACHERY MUST BE MAINTAINED.

WHO IS THE WOMAN WITH PAUL? AND THE MAN WITH THE SCARRED FACE ON THE OTHER SIDE?

THE GIRL'S FATHER MANUFACTURES STILLSUITS.

I'M TOLD THAT ONLY A FOOL WOULD BE CAUGHT IN THE DEEP DESERT WEARING ONE OF THE MAN'S SUITS.

THE SCARRED MAN IS A LATE ADDITION TO THE LIST, ARRANGED BY GURNEY AT MY REQUEST.

HE'S A SMUGGLER, ESMAR TUEK. HE'S A POWER AMONG HIS KIND. THEY ALL KNOW HIM HERE.

HE'LL SOW DOUBT AND SUSPICION JUST BY HIS PRESENCE.

HAVE YOU ARRANGED ANY OTHER LITTLE SURPRISES FOR ME?

ALL ELSE IS MOST CONVENTIONAL.

SOME QUESTION MY CHANGING OF THE LAVING BASIN CUSTOM. THIS IS MY WAY OF TELLING YOU THAT **MANY** THINGS WILL CHANGE.

I GIVE YOU A TOAST.

HERE I AM, AND HERE I WILL REMAIN!

BUT THAT WAS CLEAN, POTABLE WATER!

LET THE DINNER COMMENCE.

♫ REVIEW, FRIENDS—TROOPS LONG PAST REVIEW. ALL TO FATE A WEIGHT OF PAINS AND DOLLARS.

THEIR SPIRITS WEAR OUR SILVER COLLARS. REVIEW, FRIENDS—TROOPS LONG PAST REVIEW... ♫

I MUST COMPLIMENT YOU ON THE WINE AND YOUR CHEF, LADY JESSICA. SUPERB!

WE BROUGHT BOTH FROM CALADAN.

AND NOT A HINT OF MELANGE IN IT. ONE GETS SO TIRED OF THE SPICE IN EVERYTHING.

I UNDERSTAND, DR. KYNES, THAT ANOTHER FACTORY CRAWLER HAS BEEN LOST TO A WORM. AND YOU WERE THERE.

I WAS THERE AS WELL. NEWS TRAVELS FAST.

THEN IT'S TRUE?

OF COURSE, IT'S TRUE! THE BLASTED CARRYALL DISAPPEARED. IT SHOULDN'T BE POSSIBLE FOR ANYTHING THAT BIG TO DISAPPEAR!

IT SHOULD NOT BE POSSIBLE! SOMETHING AS LARGE AS A CARRYALL WOULDN'T SIMPLY VANISH.

SPOTTERS CUSTOMARILY KEEP THEIR EYES ON THE SAND, WATCHING FOR WORMSIGN. IF ONE OR MORE OF THE CARRYALL'S CREW WERE IN THE PAY OF THE DUKE'S FOES...

AH-H-H, I SEE.

THE GUILD BANKER...HE IS A HARKONNEN SPY. I CAN READ THE SIGNS.

DOES THIS MEAN THE GUILD ITSELF HAS TURNED AGAINST HOUSE ATREIDES?

IT MIGHT HAVE BEEN FREMEN TREACHERY.

IT'S SAID THAT THE FREMEN SCUM DRINK THE BLOOD OF THEIR DEAD.

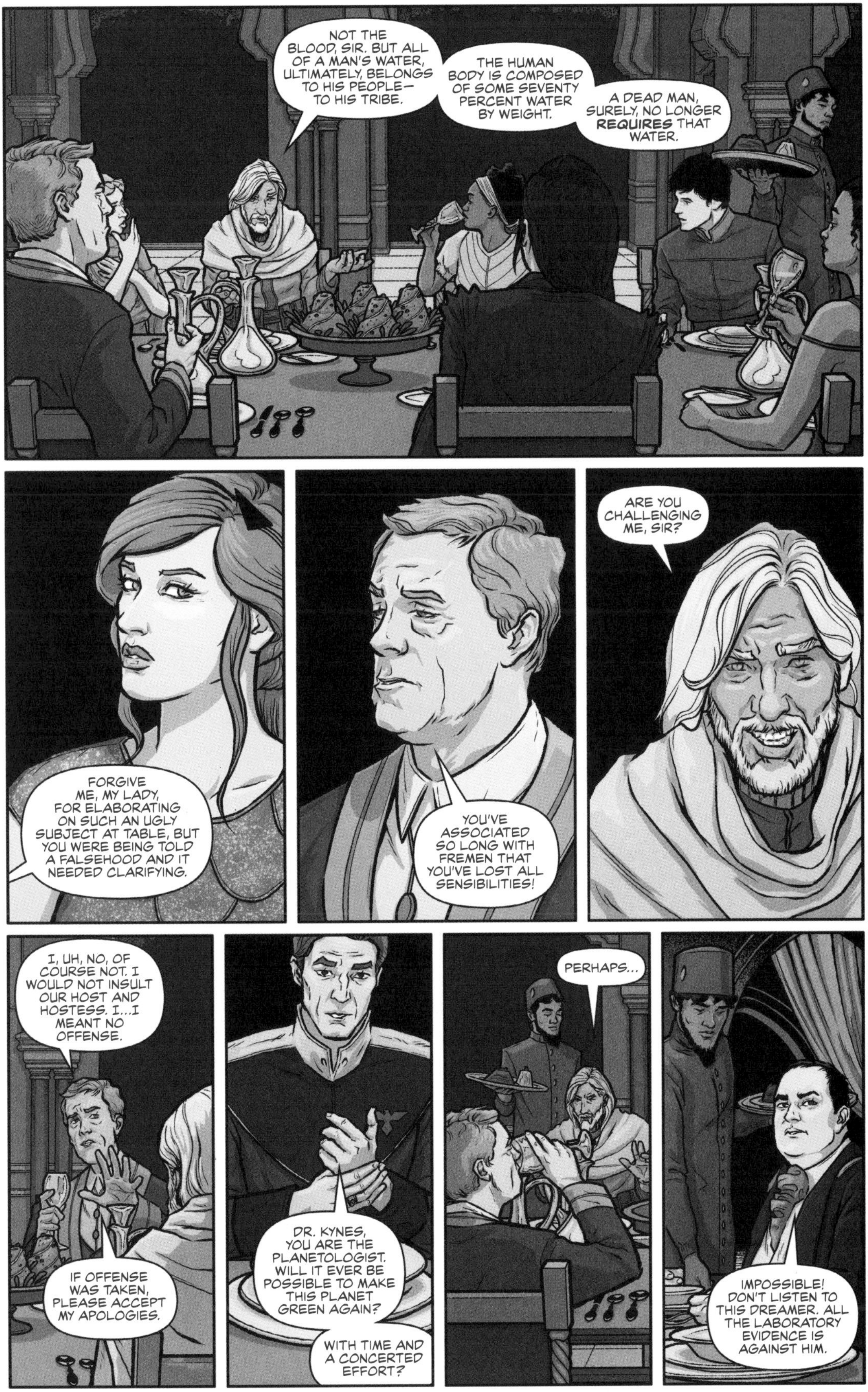
NOT THE BLOOD, SIR. BUT ALL OF A MAN'S WATER, ULTIMATELY, BELONGS TO HIS PEOPLE— TO HIS TRIBE.
THE HUMAN BODY IS COMPOSED OF SOME SEVENTY PERCENT WATER BY WEIGHT.
A DEAD MAN, SURELY, NO LONGER **REQUIRES** THAT WATER.
FORGIVE ME, MY LADY, FOR ELABORATING ON SUCH AN UGLY SUBJECT AT TABLE, BUT YOU WERE BEING TOLD A FALSEHOOD AND IT NEEDED CLARIFYING.
YOU'VE ASSOCIATED SO LONG WITH FREMEN THAT YOU'VE LOST ALL SENSIBILITIES!
ARE YOU CHALLENGING ME, SIR?
I, UH, NO, OF COURSE NOT. I WOULD NOT INSULT OUR HOST AND HOSTESS. I...I MEANT NO OFFENSE.
IF OFFENSE WAS TAKEN, PLEASE ACCEPT MY APOLOGIES.
DR. KYNES, YOU ARE THE PLANETOLOGIST. WILL IT EVER BE POSSIBLE TO MAKE THIS PLANET GREEN AGAIN?
WITH TIME AND A CONCERTED EFFORT?
PERHAPS...
IMPOSSIBLE! DON'T LISTEN TO THIS DREAMER. ALL THE LABORATORY EVIDENCE IS AGAINST HIM.

LABORATORY EVIDENCE TENDS TO BLIND US TO A VERY SIMPLE FACT.

IF WE CAN GET THREE PERCENT OF THE GREEN PLANT ELEMENT ON ARRAKIS INVOLVED, WE CAN CREATE A SELF-SUSTAINING SYSTEM.

PLEASE, EXCUSE ME.

STAY SEATED, EVERYONE. YOU WILL HAVE TO FORGIVE ME, BUT A MATTER HAS ARISEN THAT REQUIRES MY PERSONAL ATTENTION.

PAUL, TAKE OVER AS HOST FOR ME, IF YOU PLEASE. GURNEY, TAKE PAUL'S PLACE AT TABLE.

WHEN THE DINNER'S OVER, I MAY WANT YOU TO BRING PAUL TO THE FIELD C.P. WAIT FOR MY CALL.

THERE'S NO NEED FOR ALARM, BUT I MUST ASK THAT NO ONE LEAVE UNTIL OUR HOUSE GUARD SAYS IT'S SAFE.

YOU WILL BE PERFECTLY SECURE AS LONG AS YOU REMAIN HERE, AND WE'LL HAVE THIS LITTLE TROUBLE CLEARED UP VERY SHORTLY.

MY FATHER IS USING THE CODE WORDS. THIS IS A SECURITY PROBLEM, NOT ACTIVE VIOLENCE.

PLEASE GO ON WITH YOUR DINNER. I BELIEVE DR. KYNES WAS DISCUSSING WATER.

ONCE, ON CALADAN, I SAW THE BODY OF A DROWNED FISHERMAN RECOVERED.

DROWNED?

IMMERSED IN WATER UNTIL DEAD. DROWNED. QUITE THE OPPOSITE CIRCUMSTANCE FROM WHAT ONE ENCOUNTERS ON ARRAKIS.

WHAT AN INTERESTING WAY TO DIE.

ANOTHER DROWNING FISHERMAN HAD TRIED TO STAND ON THIS POOR FELLOW'S SHOULDERS IN AN ATTEMPT TO REACH UP TO THE SURFACE— TO REACH AIR.

THE INTERESTING PART WAS THE WOUNDS ON HIS SHOULDERS, MADE BY A FISHERMAN'S CLAW—BOOTS.

AND WHY IS THAT INTERESTING?

MY FATHER SAID THE DROWNING MAN WHO CLIMBS ON YOUR SHOULDERS TO SAVE HIMSELF IS UNDERSTANDABLE...

EXCEPT WHEN YOU SEE IT HAPPEN AT THE DINNER TABLE.

IS IT ATREIDES CUSTOM TO INSULT THEIR GUESTS?

HO-HO-HO-O-O-O! I'LL GIVE YOU A TOAST. TO YOUNG PAUL ATREIDES, STILL A LAD BY HIS LOOKS, BUT A MAN BY HIS ACTIONS.

ONE BAITS AN ATREIDES AT HIS OWN RISK.

MY SON MAKES A GENERAL STATEMENT AND YOU THINK HE IS TALKING ABOUT YOU? WHAT A FASCINATING REVELATION.

WE MUST LEARN THIS HARKONNEN CREATURE'S GAME. IS HE HERE TO TRY FOR PAUL? DOES HE HAVE HELP?

IN OUR SOCIETY, PEOPLE SHOULDN'T BE QUICK TO TAKE OFFENSE.

IT'S FREQUENTLY SUICIDAL.

ISN'T ANOTHER APOLOGY IN ORDER?

LADY JESSICA, I FEAR I'VE OVERINDULGED IN YOUR WINES.

YOU SERVE POTENT DRINK AT TABLE, AND I'M NOT ACCUSTOMED TO IT.

MY LADY...

OUR DUKE SENDS HIS REASSURANCES. THE MISSING CARRYALL HAS BEEN FOUND.

A HARKONNEN AGENT IN THE CREW OVERPOWERED THE OTHERS AND FLEW THE MACHINE TO A SMUGGLERS' BASE, HOPING TO SELL IT THERE.

BOTH MAN AND MACHINE WERE TURNED OVER TO OUR FORCES.

THANK YOU, ESMAR TUEK.

THE SMUGGLERS ARE VALUABLE ALLIES, MY LADY.

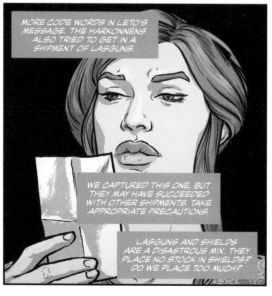

MORE CODE WORDS IN LETO'S MESSAGE. THE HARKONNENS ALSO TRIED TO GET IN A SHIPMENT OF LASGUNS.

WE CAPTURED THIS ONE, BUT THEY MAY HAVE SUCCEEDED WITH OTHER SHIPMENTS. TAKE APPROPRIATE PRECAUTIONS.

LASGUNS AND SHIELDS ARE A DISASTROUS MIX. THEY PLACE NO STOCK IN SHIELDS? DO WE PLACE TOO MUCH?

I NEVER DOUBTED WE'D FIND THE CARRYALL. ONCE MY FATHER MOVES TO SOLVE A PROBLEM, HE SOLVES IT.

THIS IS A FACT THE HARKONNENS ARE BEGINNING TO DISCOVER.

THAT NIGHT.

SOUNDS IN THE HALL... A DISTURBANCE.

LETO IS STILL IN THE COMMAND POST.

IS THIS THE HARKONNEN ATTACK?

BRING YUEH! WHERE IS DR. YUEH?

DR. YUEH? WHAT IF LETO IS HURT?

MY SWORD WAS FIRS' BLOODED ON GRUMMAN!

DUNCAN IDAHO! YOU'RE DRUNK!

103

YOU SEE WHAT YOU DID? YOU WOKE THE LADY JESSICA.

SO WHAT...

HE HAS HAD TOO MUCH SPICE BEER, MY LADY.

WE DIDN'T KNOW WHAT TO DO WITH HIM. HE WAS CREATING A DISTURBANCE OUTSIDE THE RESIDENCY, AND WE DIDN'T WANT THE LOCALS TO SEE HIM.

WOULD GIVE A BAD NAME TO HOUSE ATREIDES, MY LADY.

I WANNA KNOW WHY'M I HERE. WHAT KINNA PLACE IS THIS?

THE GOOD DOCKER! MAKIN' UH DAMN FOOL UH M'SELF, HUH?

THERE'S NO REASON FOR YOU TO STAY, MY LADY. LET ME TAKE CARE OF THIS.

SPICE BEER IS HIGHLY POTENT. MANY OF OUR MEN AREN'T ACCUSTOMED TO IT. THIS ISN'T THE FIRST CASE I'VE SEEN.

THIS IS NO WAY TO ACT IN YOUR DUKE'S HOME.

I DO NOT TAKE ORDERS FROM A DAMN HARKONNEN SPY.

HARKONNEN SPY...?

HE ACCUSES ME OF BEING A HARKONNEN SPY, IN MY OWN HOUSE! YOU KNEW OF THIS?

THERE WERE... RUMORS, MY LADY.

NOTHING MORE. EVERYONE IS SUSPICIOUS.

HAWAT! I WANT THUFIR HAWAT BROUGHT TO MY ROOMS IMMEDIATELY!

THIS IS THE MENTAT'S DOING. SUSPICION SUCH AS THIS COULD COME FROM NO OTHER SOURCE.

LOCK HIM IN ONE OF THE GUEST ROOMS. LET HIM SLEEP IT OFF.

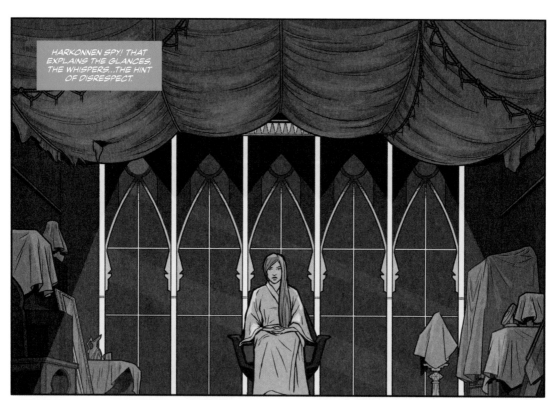

HARKONNEN SPY! THAT EXPLAINS THE GLANCES, THE WHISPERS...THE HINT OF DISRESPECT.

HAWAT! COULD HE BE THE ONE THE HARKONNENS BOUGHT?

WE SHALL SEE.

YOU SUMMONED ME, MY LADY?

BRING THAT CHAIR AND SIT FACING ME.

IT'S LONG PAST TIME TO CLEAR THE AIR BETWEEN US.

WHAT TROUBLES MY LADY?

DON'T PLAY COY WITH ME! SHALL WE BE AT LEAST THAT HONEST WITH EACH OTHER?

FIRST, YOU WILL ANSWER ME ONE QUESTION. ARE YOU A HARKONNEN AGENT?

YOU DARE INSULT ME SO?

I HAVE SERVED THREE GENERATIONS OF HOUSE ATREIDES.

SO, IT ISN'T HAWAT. I CAN TELL FROM HIS DEMEANOR, HIS MANNERISMS.

SIT DOWN. YOU INSULTED ME IN THE SAME WAY, NOW I KNOW YOU REMAIN LOYAL TO MY DUKE.

I'M PREPARED, THEREFORE, TO FORGIVE YOUR AFFRONT TO ME.

IS THERE SOMETHING TO FORGIVE?

SHALL I PLAY MY TRUMP? SHALL I TELL HIM OF THE DUKE'S DAUGHTER I'VE CARRIED WITHIN ME THESE FEW WEEKS?

NO... LETO HIMSELF DOESN'T KNOW.

THE RUMORS HAVE SOME BASIS. IS THERE A TRAITOR AMONG US? I'VE STUDIED OUR PEOPLE WITH GREAT CARE. WHO COULD IT BE? NOT GURNEY. CERTAINLY NOT DUNCAN.

IT'S NOT YOU, THUFIR. IT CANNOT BE PAUL. I KNOW IT'S NOT ME. DR. YUEH, THEN? SHALL I CALL HIM IN AND PUT HIM TO THE TEST?

YUEH? YOU KNOW THAT'S AN EMPTY GESTURE. HE'S CONDITIONED BY THE HIGH COLLEGE. THAT I KNOW FOR CERTAIN.

NOT TO MENTION THAT HIS WIFE WAS A BENE GESSERIT SLAIN BY THE HARKONNENS.

HAVEN'T YOU HEARD THE HATE IN HIS VOICE WHEN HE SPEAKS THE HARKONNEN NAME?

SO THAT'S WHAT HAPPENED TO HER.

IF YOU'RE INNOCENT, YOU'LL HAVE MY MOST ABJECT APOLOGIES.

USE YOUR MENTAT ABILITIES. WHAT IF THERE IS NO TRAITOR? THE THREAT COULD BE SOMETHING ELSE.

YOU AND I, THUFIR, OF ALL THOSE WHO LOVE THE DUKE, ARE MOST IDEALLY SITUATED TO DESTROY THE OTHER'S PLACE.

SAPPHO JUICE, TO HONE THE ABILITIES OF A MENTAT.

COULD I NOT WHISPER SUSPICIONS ABOUT YOU INTO THE DUKE'S EAR AT NIGHT?

DO YOU QUESTION MY ABILITIES? YOU THINK NOW TO TEACH ME MY TRADE?

108

WHY DON'T YOU TRUST ME?

YOU LISTEN RESPECTFULLY TO ME IN COUNCIL, YET YOU SELDOM HEED MY ADVICE. WHY?

I DON'T TRUST YOUR BENE GESSERIT MOTIVES. I KNOW SOMETHING OF THE **REAL** TRAINING THEY GIVE YOU.

I'VE SEEN IT COME OUT IN PAUL. WITCHES...

YOU POOR FOOL, THUFIR! WHATEVER RUMORS YOU'VE HEARD ABOUT OUR SCHOOLS, THE TRUTH IS **FAR** GREATER.

IF I WISHED TO DESTROY THE DUKE...OR YOU, OR ANY OTHER PERSON WITHIN MY REACH, YOU COULD NOT STOP ME.

POISON DARTS HIDDEN IN HIS SLEEVES.

I KNOW THE SECRET WEAPONS HE CARRIES...

LET US PRAY VIOLENCE SHALL NEVER BE NECESSARY BETWEEN US.

YOUR LOYALTY TO THE DUKE IS ALL THAT GUARANTEES YOUR SAFETY WITH ME.

YOU HAVE FAILED ONCE BEFORE, THUFIR HAWAT. YOU DID NOT DETECT A THREAT TO MY SON, AND THE HUNTER-SEEKER ALMOST KILLED HIM.

I SUBMITTED MY RESIGNATION TO THE DUKE! HE DID NOT ACCEPT IT.

SEE THAT IT DOES NOT HAPPEN AGAIN.

THERE IS A DEEPER PLOT, AND THE HARKONNENS MEAN TO TURN US AGAINST EACH OTHER.

NOW GO AND FIND OUT THE TRUTH OF WHAT IS GOING ON.

YES... MY LADY.

NOW WE'LL SEE SOME PROPER ACTION.

LATER THAT NIGHT...

A FREMEN MESSENGER DELIVERED THIS NOTE TO THE OUTER GUARD JUST AS I ARRIVED FROM THE COMMAND POST...

A column of smoke by day; a pillar of fire by night

WHAT DOES IT MEAN? I'LL SHOW THE NOTE TO HAWAT AS SOON AS I SEE HIM.

SHOULD I WAKEN JESSICA? THERE'S NO REASON TO PLAY THE SECRECY GAME WITH HER ANY LONGER.

BLAST AND DAMN THAT DUNCAN IDAHO!

NO, NOT DUNCAN. I WAS WRONG NOT TO TAKE JESSICA INTO MY CONFIDENCE FROM THE FIRST.

I MUST DO IT NOW, BEFORE MORE DAMAGE IS DONE.

A BODY! NEAR THE SHIELD GENERATOR ROOM...

A SPY? OR A FRIEND?

ESMAR TUEK! THE SMUGGLER... WHY IS HE HERE?

STABBED... HERE IN THE RESIDENCY!

HOW COULD THIS MAN BE HERE?

WHO KILLED HIM?

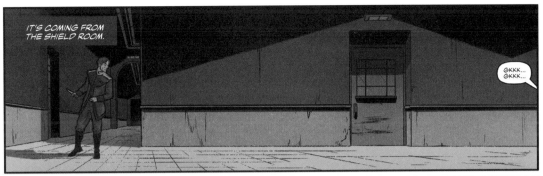

IT'S COMING FROM THE SHIELD ROOM.

GKKK... GKKK...

MAPES!

GKKKK... GKKKK, MY... LORD!

WHAT HAPPENED HERE? WHO DID THIS?

KILLED... GUARD. SENT... GET...TUEK.

ESCAPE...

M'LADY... NO.

YOU... HERE...

UUNNNHHH-HHHH.....

NO PULSE... SHE'S BEEN STABBED IN THE BACK.

WHAT IS-?

WAIT... SOMETHING—

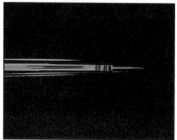

NEED MY PERSONAL SHIELD...

114

AHHH!

DART... TRANQUILIZER...

YUEH! HE'S SABOTAGED THE HOUSE GENERATORS!

WE'RE WIDE OPEN!

YUEH! HOW?

THE DRUG IN THE DART IS SELECTIVE.

YOU CAN SPEAK, BUT I'D ADVISE AGAINST IT.

IT *CAN'T* BE YUEH. HE'S CONDITIONED...

HOW?

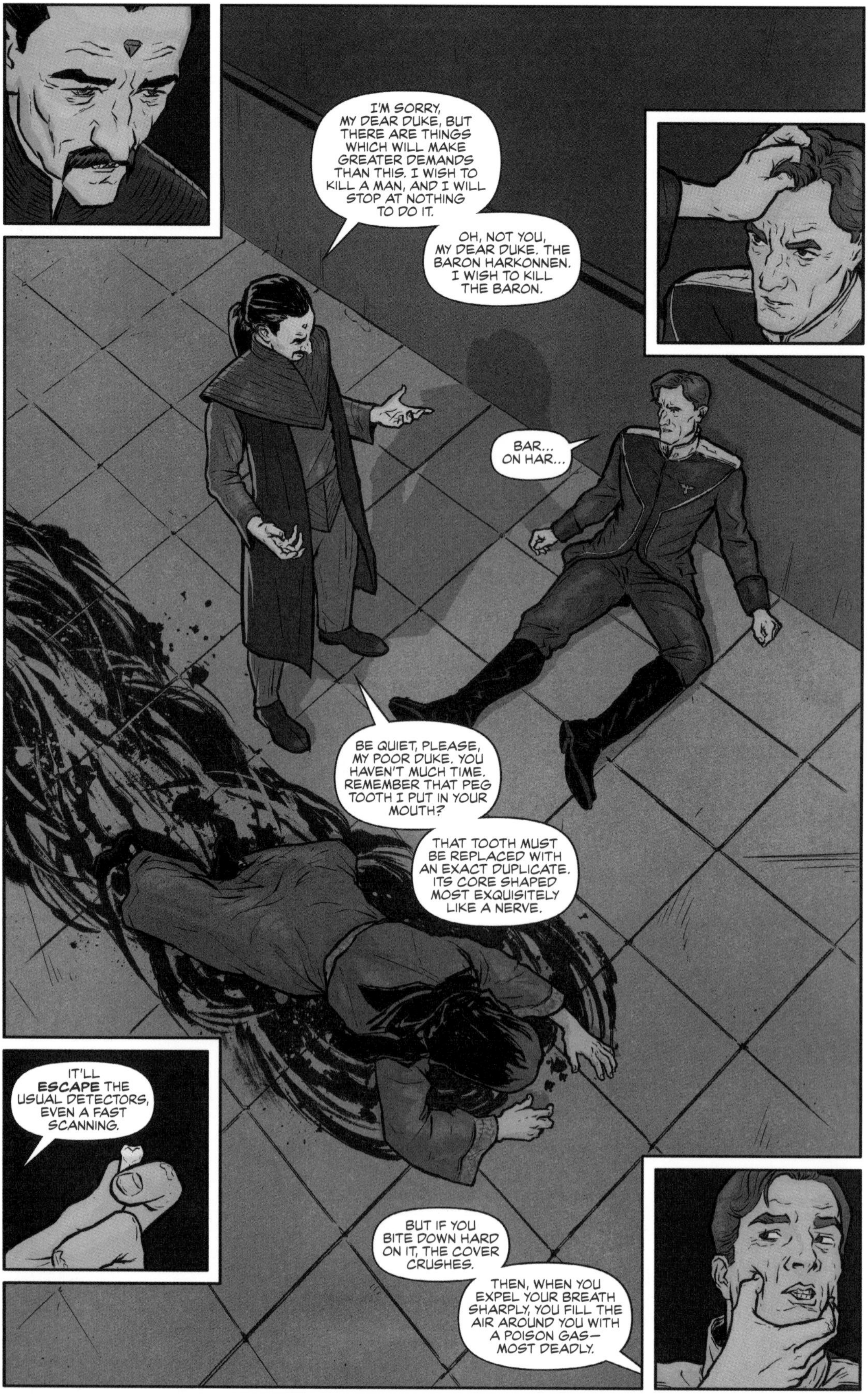
I'M SORRY, MY DEAR DUKE, BUT THERE ARE THINGS WHICH WILL MAKE GREATER DEMANDS THAN THIS. I WISH TO KILL A MAN, AND I WILL STOP AT NOTHING TO DO IT.
OH, NOT YOU, MY DEAR DUKE. THE BARON HARKONNEN. I WISH TO KILL THE BARON.
BAR... ON HAR...
BE QUIET, PLEASE, MY POOR DUKE. YOU HAVEN'T MUCH TIME. REMEMBER THAT PEG TOOTH I PUT IN YOUR MOUTH?
THAT TOOTH MUST BE REPLACED WITH AN EXACT DUPLICATE. ITS CORE SHAPED MOST EXQUISITELY LIKE A NERVE.
IT'LL **ESCAPE** THE USUAL DETECTORS, EVEN A FAST SCANNING.
BUT IF YOU BITE DOWN HARD ON IT, THE COVER CRUSHES.
THEN, WHEN YOU EXPEL YOUR BREATH SHARPLY, YOU FILL THE AIR AROUND YOU WITH A POISON GAS— MOST DEADLY.

ONLY YOU CAN DO THIS, MY POOR DUKE. YOU WERE DEAD ANYWAY, BUT YOU WILL GET CLOSE TO THE BARON BEFORE YOU DIE.

YOU WILL BE TIED, DRUGGED, AND THE BARON WILL THINK YOU'RE NO THREAT. BUT YOU WILL REMEMBER THE TOOTH.

WHY...?

YOU ARE THE PRICE OF MY SHAITAN'S BARGAIN WITH THE BARON. AND I MUST BE CERTAIN HE HAS FULFILLED HIS HALF OF IT.

WHEN I SEE HIM, I'LL KNOW. MY POOR WANNA...

REFUSE...

AH-H, NO! YOU MUSTN'T REFUSE. BECAUSE IN RETURN I WILL SAVE YOUR SON AND YOUR WOMAN.

I'LL MAKE IT APPEAR THEY'RE DEAD, SEND THEM TO SAFETY AMONG THE FREMEN. IT'S THE ONLY WAY.

FOR PAUL.

YOU'LL BE UNCONSCIOUS PRESENTLY, AND THEN I'LL DO MY WORK.

BUT YOU MUST REMEMBER...

REMEMBER THE TOOTH...

WHAT'S THAT SOUND? WHERE AM I?

WHAT TIME IS IT? LATE...

SLUGGISH... DRUGGED?

MY WRISTS...

IT HAS COME. HOW SIMPLE IT WAS TO SUBDUE THE BENE GESSERIT.

HAWAT WAS RIGHT. A TRAITOR AMONG US...

NOW I REMEMBER...

SOMEONE IN THE DARK.

WHERE IS LETO?

CALM. MUST THINK...

I SHALL NOT FEAR. FEAR IS THE MIND-KILLER...

YOU ARE AWAKE. DO NOT PRETEND.

THE DRUG WAS TIMED. WE KNEW TO THE MINUTE WHEN YOU'D COME OUT OF IT.

SUCH A PITY YOU MUST REMAIN GAGGED.

WE COULD HAVE SUCH AN INTERESTING CONVERSATION. BUT I'M AWARE OF YOUR ABILITIES.

THEY'D HAVE TO KNOW MY EXACT WEIGHT, MY METABOLISM, MY...YUEH! HE'S THE ONLY ONE IT COULD BE.

I HAVE SOMEONE TO SEE YOU, MY DEAR. COME IN, PITER.

AS YOU SAY, BARON. YOU PROMISED HER TO ME.

I HAVE A SURPRISE FOR PITER. HE THINKS HE WANTS YOU AS A REWARD, LADY JESSICA.

BUT I WISH TO DEMONSTRATE A THING: THAT HE DOES NOT REALLY WANT YOU.

YOU PLAY WITH ME, BARON?

IN MANY WAYS, PITER IS QUITE NAIVE. I KNOW WHAT HE REALLY WANTS.

PITER WANTS POWER.

YOU PROMISED I COULD HAVE HER!

I GIVE YOU A CHOICE, PITER.

TAKE THIS WOMAN AND EXILE FROM THE IMPERIUM...OR TAKE THE DUCHY OF ATREIDES ON ARRAKIS TO RULE AS YOU SEE FIT IN MY NAME.

YOU COULD BE DUKE IN ALL BUT NAME.

YOU ONLY WANT HER BECAUSE SHE'S A DUKE'S WOMAN.

YOU DO NOT JOKE WITH PITER?

IS LETO DEAD, THEN?

I'VE MADE MY CHOICE, BARON.

I WILL TAKE THE DUCHY.

AH-H, I AM NOT SURPRISED.

IS IT NOT WONDERFUL THAT I KNOW PITER SO WELL? YOU UNDERSTAND, LADY JESSICA? I HOLD NO RANCOR TOWARD YOU. IT'S A NECESSITY. MUCH BETTER THIS WAY.

AND I'VE NOT ACTUALLY ORDERED YOU DESTROYED. WHEN IT'S ASKED OF ME WHAT HAPPENED TO YOU, I CAN SHRUG IT OFF IN ALL TRUTH.

THESE GUARDS WILL FOLLOW YOUR ORDERS, PITER. WHATEVER IS DONE, I LEAVE TO YOU. I WILL HAVE NO BLOOD ON MY HANDS.

AND TRY NONE OF YOUR TRICKS, LADY JESSICA. KINET HERE IS STONE DEAF.

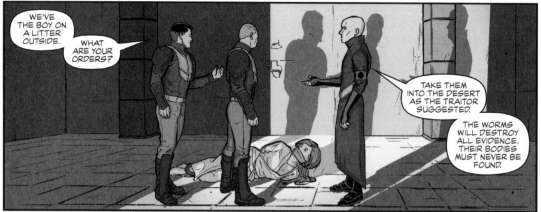

WE'VE THE BOY ON A LITTER OUTSIDE.

WHAT ARE YOUR ORDERS?

TAKE THEM INTO THE DESERT AS THE TRAITOR SUGGESTED.

THE WORMS WILL DESTROY ALL EVIDENCE. THEIR BODIES MUST NEVER BE FOUND.

YOU DON'T WISH TO DISPATCH THEM YOURSELF?

I FOLLOW MY BARON'S EXAMPLE. TAKE THEM WHERE THE TRAITOR SAID. LEAVE NO TRACE.

HE FEARS THE TRUTHSAYER, JUST LIKE THE BARON.

DROP 'EM ON THE DESERT LIKE THAT TRAITOR SAID. CUT 'EM ONCE OR TWICE, LEAVE THE EVIDENCE FOR THE WORMS.

NOTHING TO CLEAN UP AFTERWARD.

PAUL! HE'S ALIVE!

IS HE DRUGGED? NO, HE'S AWAKE. HE MUSTN'T TRY THE VOICE!

122

THIS THE 'THOPTER WE'RE SUPPOSED TO USE?

IT'S THE ONE THE TRAITOR SAID WAS FIXED FOR DESERT WORK.

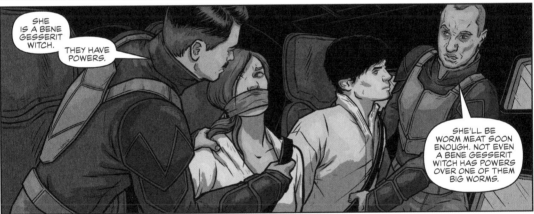

SHE IS A BENE GESSERIT WITCH.

THEY HAVE POWERS.

SHE'LL BE WORM MEAT SOON ENOUGH. NOT EVEN A BENE GESSERIT WITCH HAS POWERS OVER ONE OF THEM BIG WORMS.

I'LL KEEP AN EYE ON THESE TWO. YOU FLY OUT INTO THE DESERT. TO WHERE THE TRAITOR SAID.

THE RESTRAINT BELT HAS BEEN CUT. HAS SOMEONE BEEN AT THIS 'THOPTER, PREPARING IT FOR US?

WHO?

YUEH? BUT HE BETRAYED US!

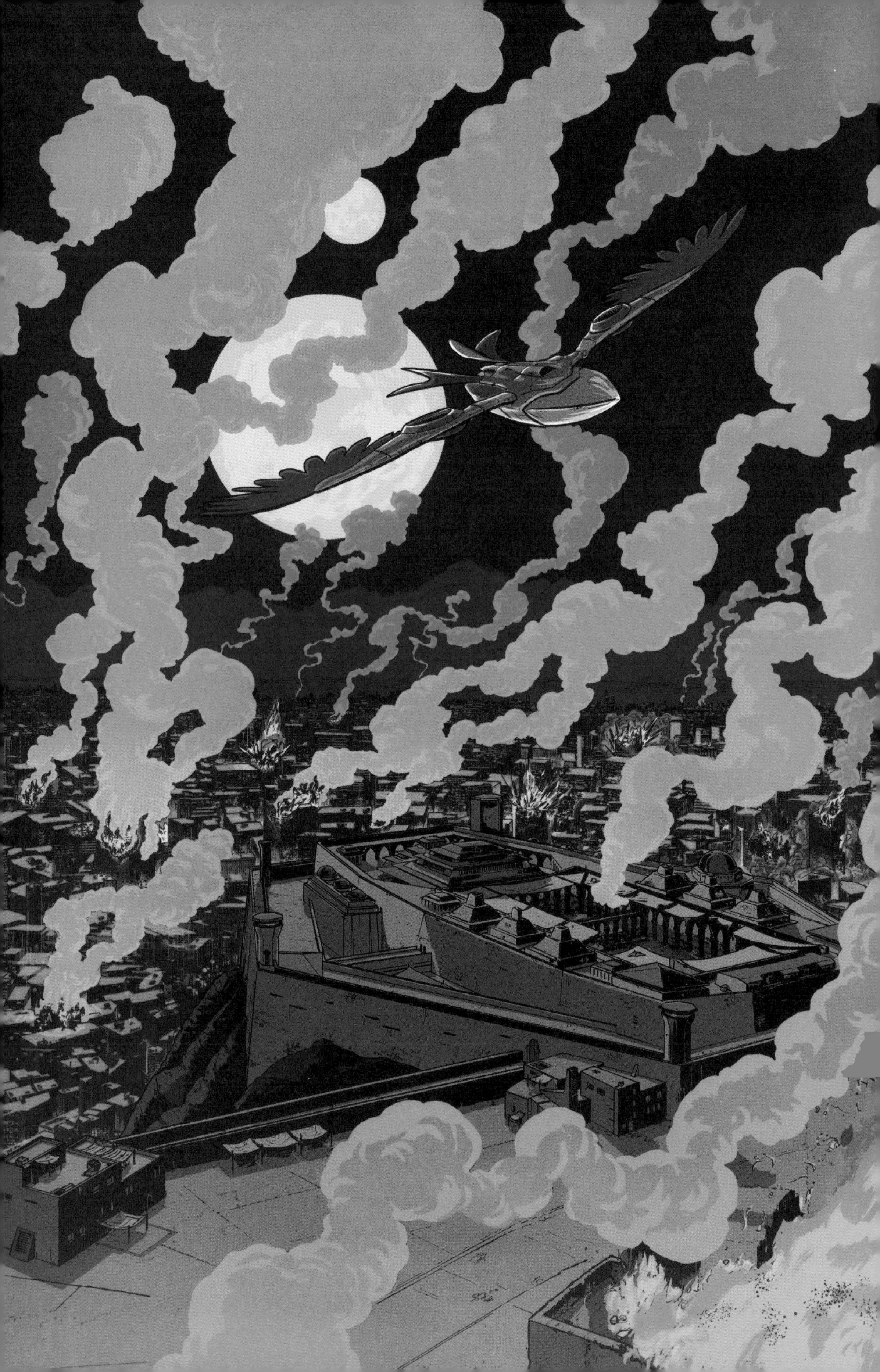

SURE DO SEEM A **SHAME** TO WASTE A GOOD-LOOKING WOMAN LIKE THIS. REAL PRETTY, SHE IS.

BENE GESSERIT AIN'T ALL HIGHBORN. YOU THINKING WHAT I THINK YOU'RE THINKING?

WHO'D BE TO KNOW?

YOU LAY A HAND ON MY MOTHER...

CUB'S GOT A BARK. AIN'T GOT NO BITE, THOUGH.

PAUL'S PITCHING HIS VOICE TOO HIGH. IT MAY WORK, THOUGH.

THIS OUGHTA BE FAR ENOUGH. THE TRAITOR SAID TO PUT 'EM ON THE SAND ANYWHERE NEAR THE SHIELD WALL.

PAUL HASN'T MASTERED THE VOICE YET. IF HE FAILS...

LET'S SEE NOW, BEFORE WE CUT YOU AND DUMP YOU ON THE SANDS...

I DUNNO, CZIGO...

AHHH, LOOK...

REMOVE HER GAG!

STOP THAT!

AWW, SHUT YOUR TRAP. HER HANDS ARE TIED.

NO NEED TO FIGHT OVER ME...

YOU MUSTN'T DISAGREE.

YEAH, NO NEED TO FIGHT—

UNNGHHHH

KKKGGGGKKK

I KNOW THAT TRICK...

NOW FOR THE CUB, SO WE CAN BE ALONE...

NO NEED FOR THAT. WOULDN'T YOU RATHER HAVE ME COOPERATIVE?

GIVE THE BOY A CHANCE OUT THERE IN THAT SAND...YOU COULD FIND YOURSELF WELL REWARDED.

YOU'RE TRYING TO TRICK ME.

I DON'T WANT TO SEE MY SON DIE. IS THAT A TRICK?

ALL RIGHT, GO. OUT INTO THE DESERT...

THOUGH YOU MAY FIND THE KNIFE A KINDNESS...

UNNNHHHH!

PAUL'S TRAINING...

PRECISE POSITIONING OF THE BLOW, THROUGH THE DIAPHRAGM TO CRUSH THE RIGHT VENTRICLE OF THE HEART.

HE'S ALREADY DEAD.

THAT WAS A FOOLISH RISK. I COULD HAVE HANDLED HIM.

I SAW THE OPENING AND I USED IT.

DID YOU SEE YUEH'S HOUSE SIGN SCRATCHED ON THE CEILING OF THE 'THOPTER? THERE'S A PACKAGE HIDDEN UNDER THE SEAT.

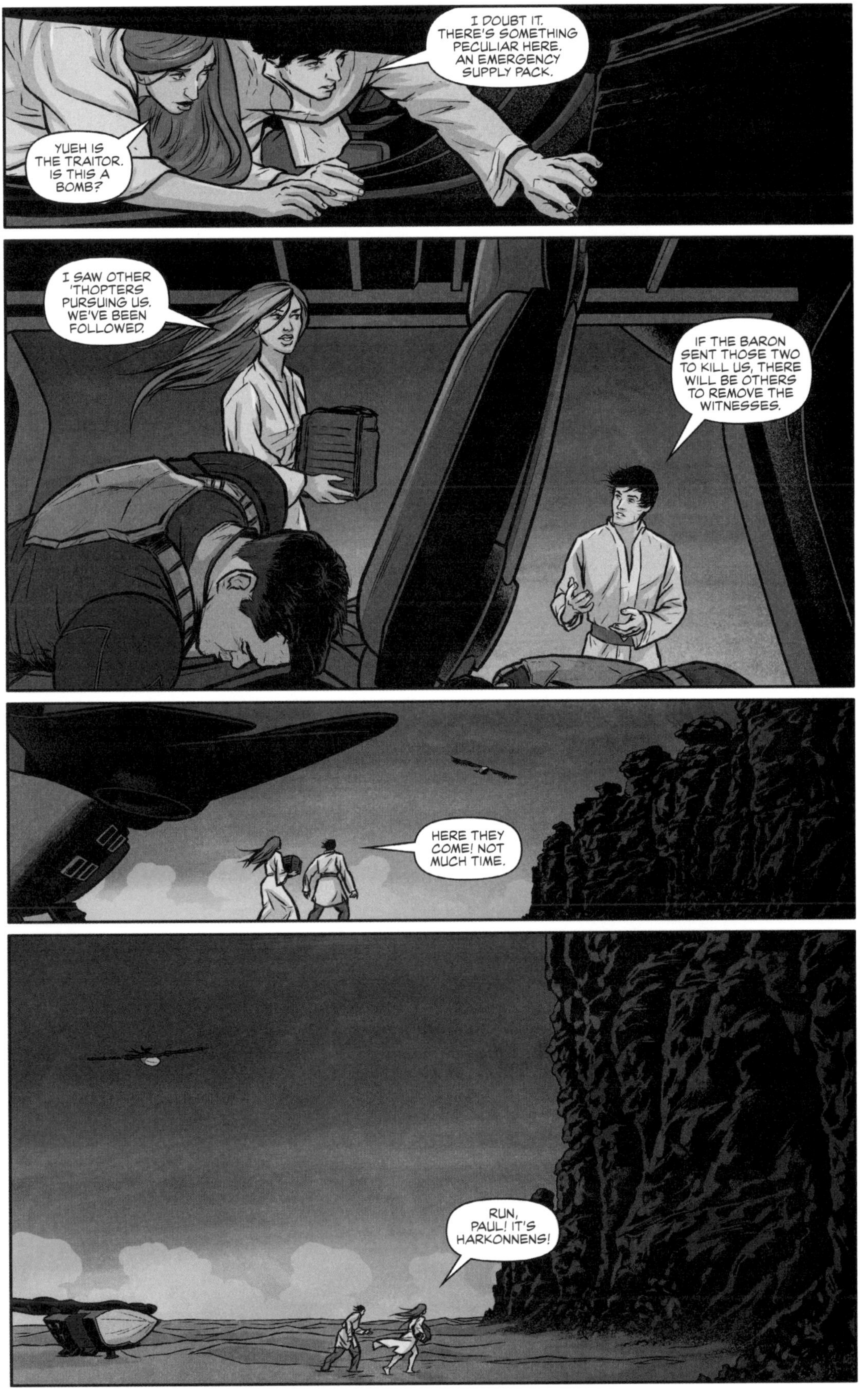
I DOUBT IT. THERE'S SOMETHING PECULIAR HERE. AN EMERGENCY SUPPLY PACK.
YUEH IS THE TRAITOR. IS THIS A BOMB?
I SAW OTHER 'THOPTERS PURSUING US. WE'VE BEEN FOLLOWED.
IF THE BARON SENT THOSE TWO TO KILL US, THERE WILL BE OTHERS TO REMOVE THE WITNESSES.
HERE THEY COME! NOT MUCH TIME.
RUN, PAUL! IT'S HARKONNENS!

YOU'RE YUEH, THE TRAITOR. YOU CAN RELAX NOW. WHEN YOU DROPPED THE HOUSE SHIELDS WE CAME RIGHT IN.

EVERYTHING'S UNDER CONTROL HERE. IS THIS THE DUKE?

ARRAKEEN RESIDENCY.

THIS IS THE DUKE.

HE'S WEARING A HARKONNEN UNIFORM, BUT HE'S A SARDAUKAR. ONE OF THE EMPEROR'S ELITE TROOPS. THE ARROGANT MANNER IS UNMISTAKABLE.

DEAD?

MERELY UNCONSCIOUS. I SUGGEST YOU TIE HIM. HE'LL AWAKEN IN TWO HOURS OR SO.

A LITTLE SOUVENIR. WHERE'S THE DUCAL SIGNET RING?

HE DOESN'T HAVE IT ON HIM. HE MAY HAVE SENT IT WITH A MESSENGER AT SOME POINT.

THEY MUST NOT KNOW THAT I HID THE DUKE'S RING IN THE PACK ON THE 'THOPTER. PAUL MUST FIND IT...

HE'LL BE DELIVERED TO THE BARON ALL PROPERLY TRUSSED LIKE A ROAST FOR THE OVEN.

THIS WAS NOTHING TO FEAR EVEN WHEN AWAKE.

GO. WE'VE NO MORE TIME FOR CHITCHAT, TRAITOR. YOU'RE KNOWN; YOU'LL BE SAFE ENOUGH IN THE HALLS.

TRAITOR...

TRAITOR...THAT IS ALL
I WILL EVER BE. BUT,
I DID IT FOR WANNA...

DUNCAN IDAHO MUST
NOT FAIL ME...

TRAITOR!
THE BARON WILL
WANT TO SEE
YOU SOON.

IF DUNCAN IDAHO SUSPECTS ME, IF HE DOESN'T WAIT AND GO EXACTLY WHERE I TOLD HIM... JESSICA AND PAUL WILL NOT BE SAVED FROM THE CARNAGE.

I'LL BE DENIED EVEN THE **SMALLEST** RELIEF FROM MY ACT.

HOW CONFIDENT THEY ARE...

YOU, WAIT OVER THERE, OUT OF THE WAY. WAIT FOR THE BARON.

AND THE BARON—HE WILL ENCOUNTER A SMALL TOOTH.

THE BATTLE CONTINUES, BUT SOON ARRAKEEN WILL FALL.

HARKONNEN COMMAND SHIP.

THEN I CAN MOVE INTO THE RESIDENCY, RATHER THAN THIS LANDED LIGHTER AS MY COMMAND CENTER.

MY OWN HARKONNEN TROOPS, AS WELL AS THE CRACK IMPERIAL SARDAUKAR IN MY HOUSE LIVERY.

THE ATREIDES WON'T STAND A CHANCE.

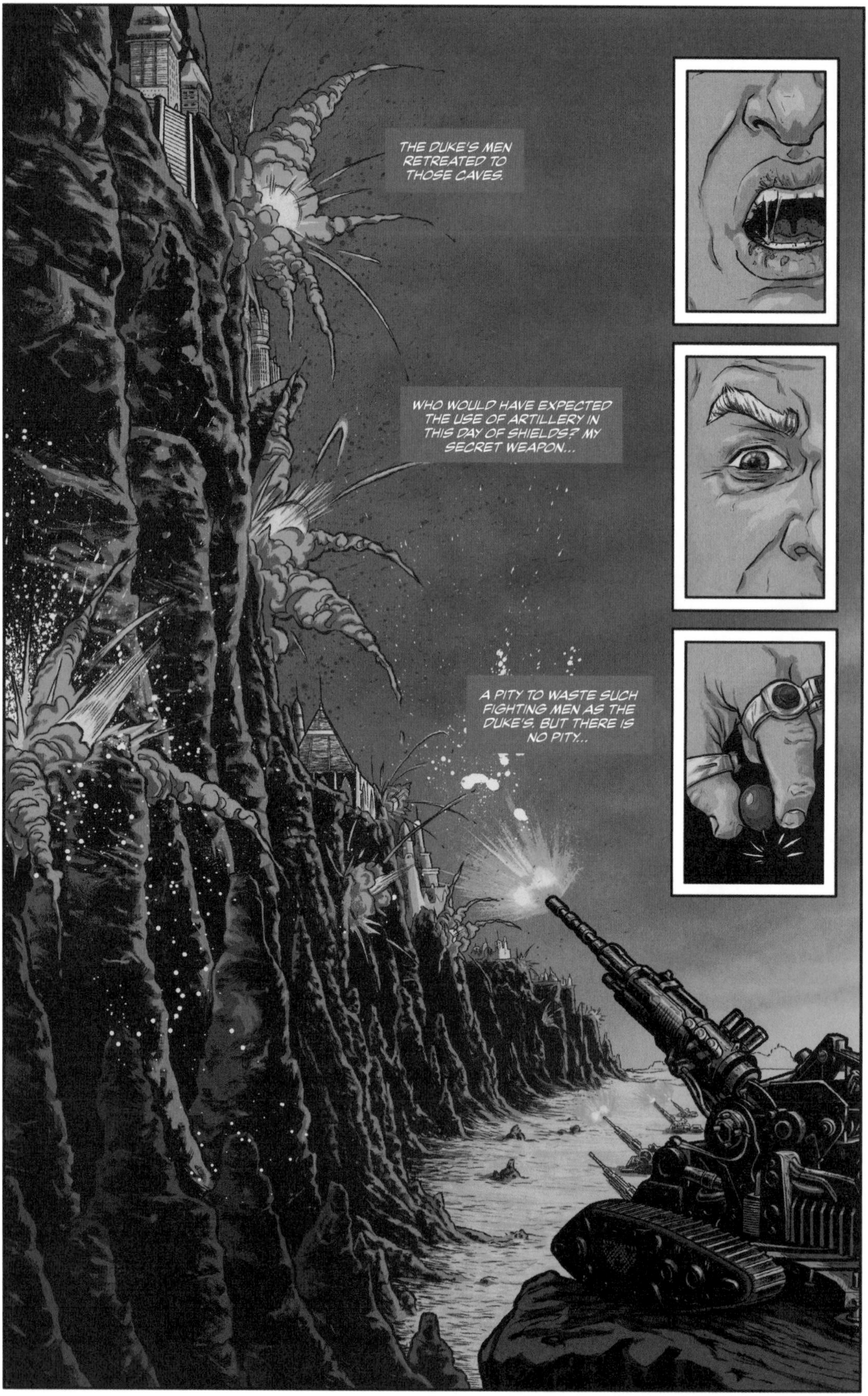

THE DUKE'S MEN RETREATED TO THOSE CAVES.
WHO WOULD HAVE EXPECTED THE USE OF ARTILLERY IN THIS DAY OF SHIELDS? MY SECRET WEAPON...
A PITY TO WASTE SUCH FIGHTING MEN AS THE DUKE'S. BUT THERE IS NO PITY...

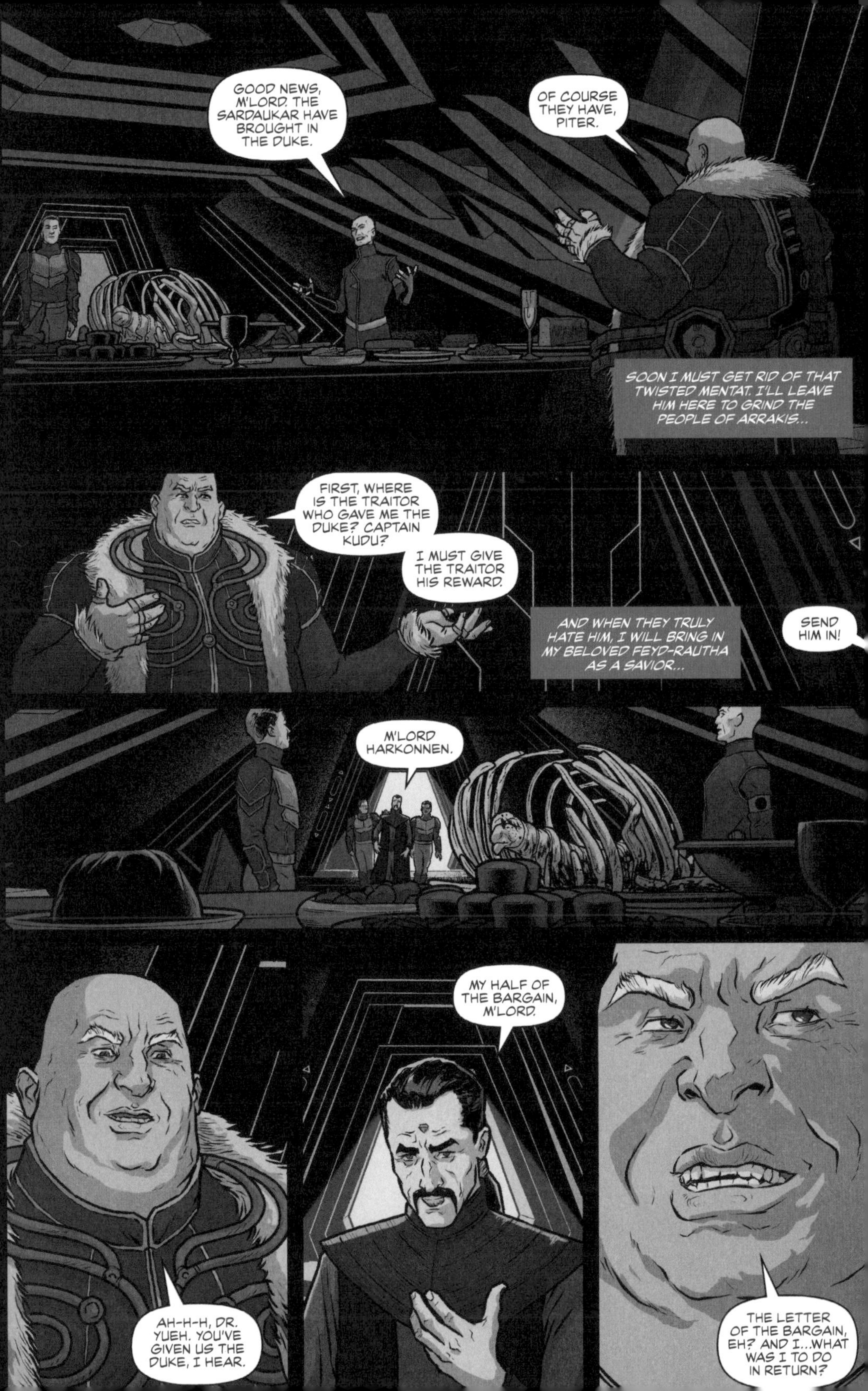
GOOD NEWS, M'LORD. THE SARDAUKAR HAVE BROUGHT IN THE DUKE.
OF COURSE THEY HAVE, PITER.
SOON I MUST GET RID OF THAT TWISTED MENTAT. I'LL LEAVE HIM HERE TO GRIND THE PEOPLE OF ARRAKIS...
FIRST, WHERE IS THE TRAITOR WHO GAVE ME THE DUKE? CAPTAIN KUDU?
I MUST GIVE THE TRAITOR HIS REWARD.
AND WHEN THEY TRULY HATE HIM, I WILL BRING IN MY BELOVED FEYD-RAUTHA AS A SAVIOR...
SEND HIM IN!
M'LORD HARKONNEN.
AH-H-H, DR. YUEH. YOU'VE GIVEN US THE DUKE, I HEAR.
MY HALF OF THE BARGAIN, M'LORD.
THE LETTER OF THE BARGAIN, EH? AND I...WHAT WAS I TO DO IN RETURN?

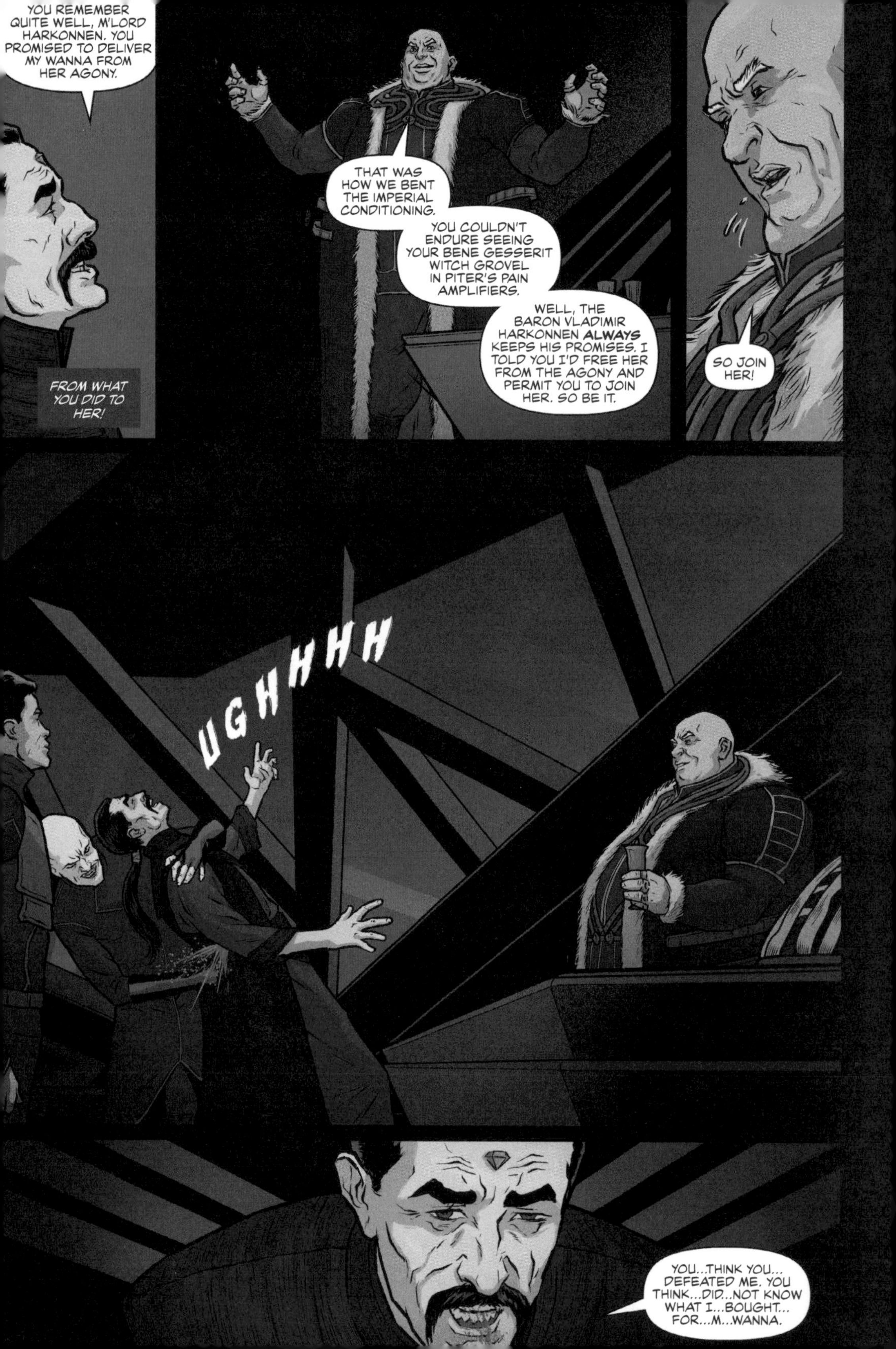

YOU REMEMBER QUITE WELL, M'LORD HARKONNEN. YOU PROMISED TO DELIVER MY WANNA FROM HER AGONY.
FROM WHAT YOU DID TO HER!
THAT WAS HOW WE BENT THE IMPERIAL CONDITIONING.
YOU COULDN'T ENDURE SEEING YOUR BENE GESSERIT WITCH GROVEL IN PITER'S PAIN AMPLIFIERS.
WELL, THE BARON VLADIMIR HARKONNEN ALWAYS KEEPS HIS PROMISES. I TOLD YOU I'D FREE HER FROM THE AGONY AND PERMIT YOU TO JOIN HER. SO BE IT.
SO JOIN HER!
UGHHHHH
YOU...THINK YOU... DEFEATED ME. YOU THINK...DID...NOT KNOW WHAT I...BOUGHT... FOR...M...WANNA.

I NEVER COULD BRING MYSELF TO TRUST A TRAITOR. NOT EVEN A TRAITOR I CREATED. HE DID GIVE US THE DUKE?

OF A CERTAINTY, MY LORD.

THEN GET HIM IN HERE!

WHAT DID THE TRAITOR MEAN WHEN HE SAID "YOU THINK YOU DEFEATED ME"?

WELL, MY DEAR DUKE!

I HAVE WAITED SO LONG FOR THIS MOMENT. HAS IT LOST SOME OF ITS SAVOR?

I BELIEVE THE GOOD DUKE IS DRUGGED. THAT'S HOW YUEH CAUGHT HIM FOR US.

AREN'T YOU DRUGGED, MY DEAR DUKE?

DAMN THAT CURSED DOCTOR THROUGH ALL ETERNITY!

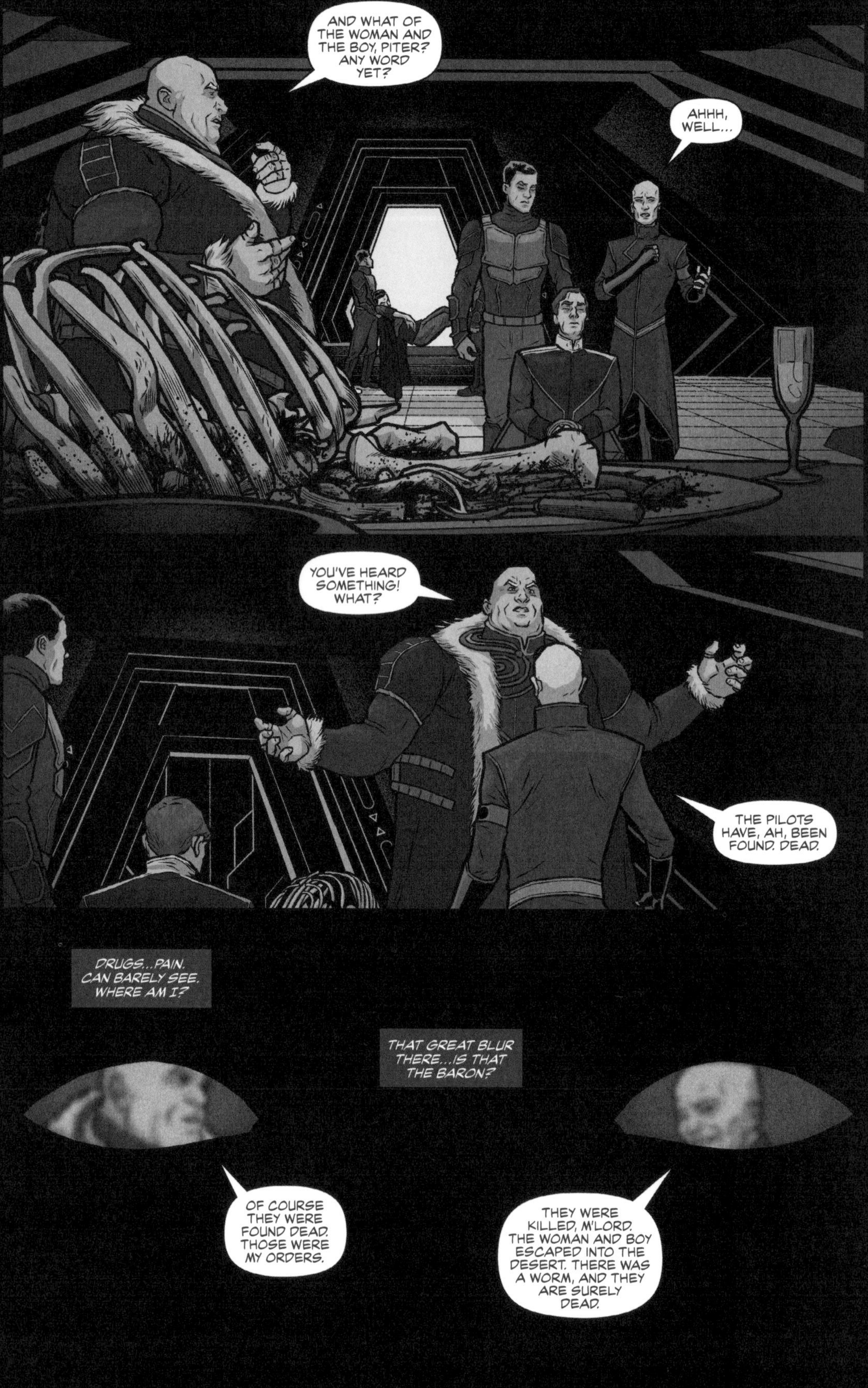
AND WHAT OF THE WOMAN AND THE BOY, PITER? ANY WORD YET?
AHHH, WELL...
YOU'VE HEARD SOMETHING! WHAT?
THE PILOTS HAVE, AH, BEEN FOUND. DEAD.
DRUGS...PAIN. CAN BARELY SEE. WHERE AM I?
THAT GREAT BLUR THERE...IS THAT THE BARON?
OF COURSE THEY WERE FOUND DEAD. THOSE WERE MY ORDERS.
THEY WERE KILLED, M'LORD. THE WOMAN AND BOY ESCAPED INTO THE DESERT. THERE WAS A WORM, AND THEY ARE SURELY DEAD.

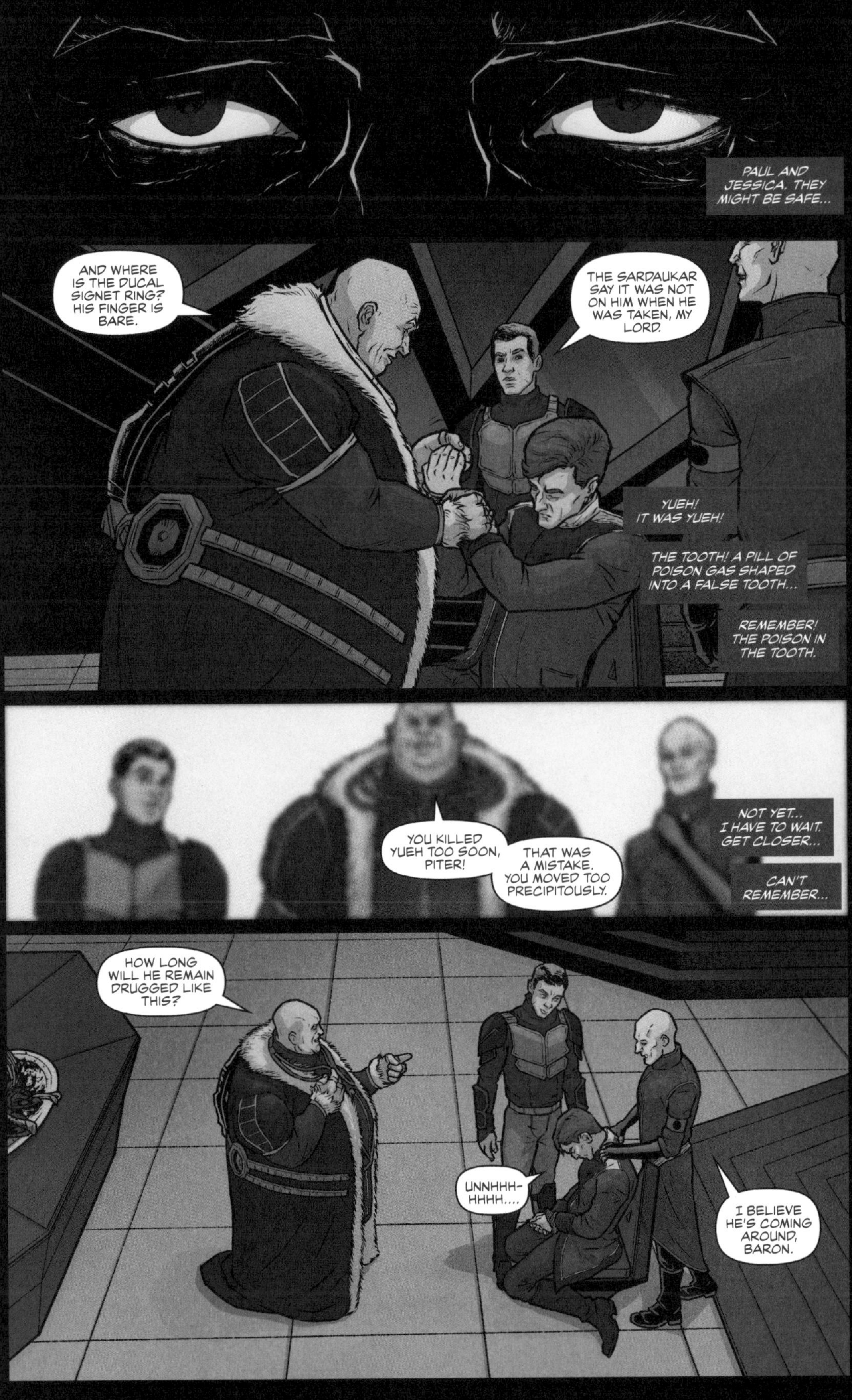
PAUL AND JESSICA. THEY MIGHT BE SAFE...
AND WHERE IS THE DUCAL SIGNET RING? HIS FINGER IS BARE.
THE SARDAUKAR SAY IT WAS NOT ON HIM WHEN HE WAS TAKEN, MY LORD.
YUEH! IT WAS YUEH!
THE TOOTH! A PILL OF POISON GAS SHAPED INTO A FALSE TOOTH...
REMEMBER! THE POISON IN THE TOOTH.
YOU KILLED YUEH TOO SOON, PITER!
THAT WAS A MISTAKE. YOU MOVED TOO PRECIPITOUSLY.
NOT YET... I HAVE TO WAIT. GET CLOSER...
CAN'T REMEMBER...
HOW LONG WILL HE REMAIN DRUGGED LIKE THIS?
UNNHHH-HHHH....
I BELIEVE HE'S COMING AROUND, BARON.

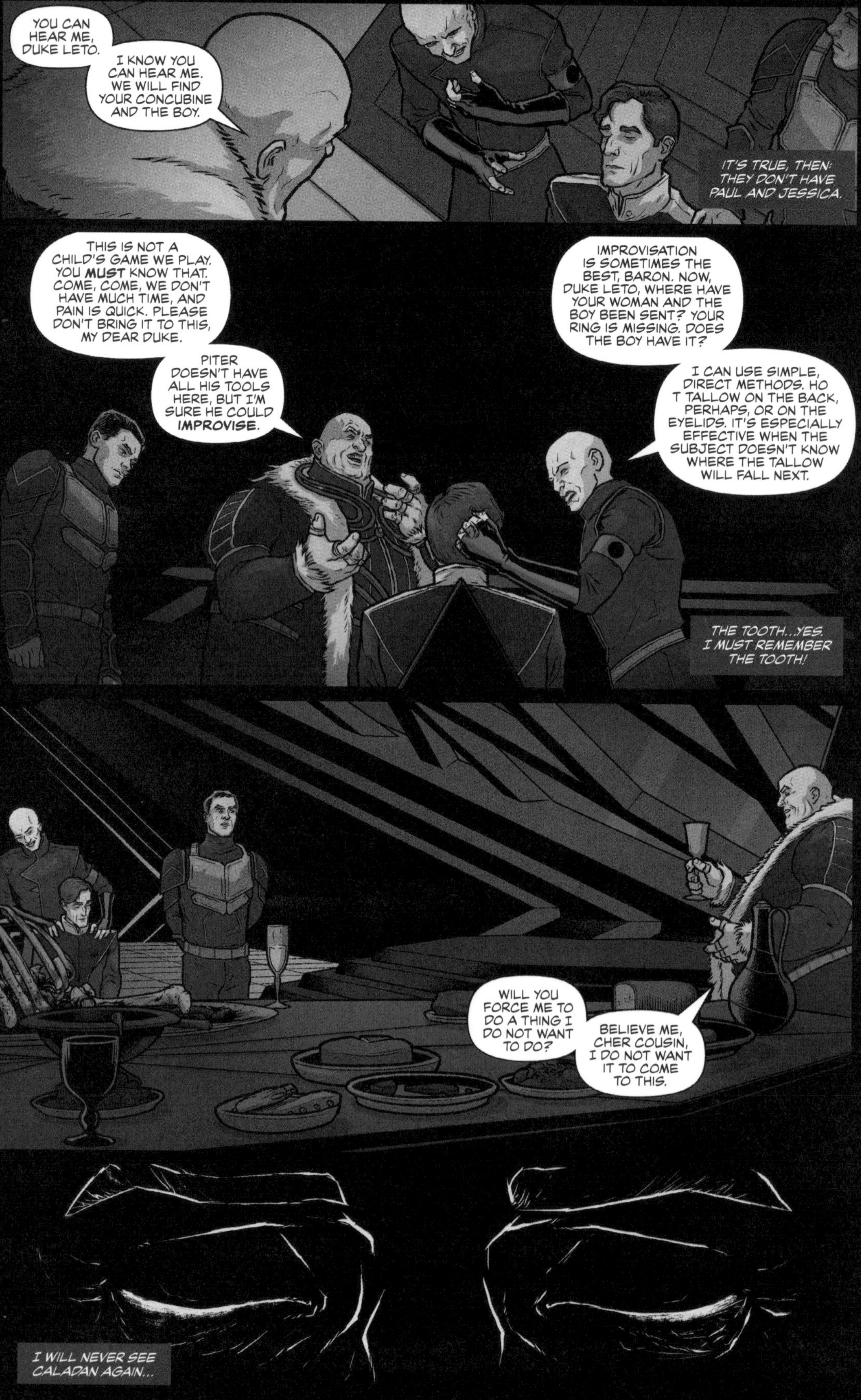

YOU CAN HEAR ME, DUKE LETO.
I KNOW YOU CAN HEAR ME. WE WILL FIND YOUR CONCUBINE AND THE BOY.
IT'S TRUE, THEN: THEY DON'T HAVE PAUL AND JESSICA.
THIS IS NOT A CHILD'S GAME WE PLAY. YOU MUST KNOW THAT. COME, COME, WE DON'T HAVE MUCH TIME, AND PAIN IS QUICK. PLEASE DON'T BRING IT TO THIS, MY DEAR DUKE.
PITER DOESN'T HAVE ALL HIS TOOLS HERE, BUT I'M SURE HE COULD IMPROVISE.
IMPROVISATION IS SOMETIMES THE BEST, BARON. NOW, DUKE LETO, WHERE HAVE YOUR WOMAN AND THE BOY BEEN SENT? YOUR RING IS MISSING. DOES THE BOY HAVE IT?
I CAN USE SIMPLE, DIRECT METHODS. HO T TALLOW ON THE BACK, PERHAPS, OR ON THE EYELIDS. IT'S ESPECIALLY EFFECTIVE WHEN THE SUBJECT DOESN'T KNOW WHERE THE TALLOW WILL FALL NEXT.
THE TOOTH...YES. I MUST REMEMBER THE TOOTH!
WILL YOU FORCE ME TO DO A THING I DO NOT WANT TO DO?
BELIEVE ME, CHER COUSIN, I DO NOT WANT IT TO COME TO THIS.
I WILL NEVER SEE CALADAN AGAIN...

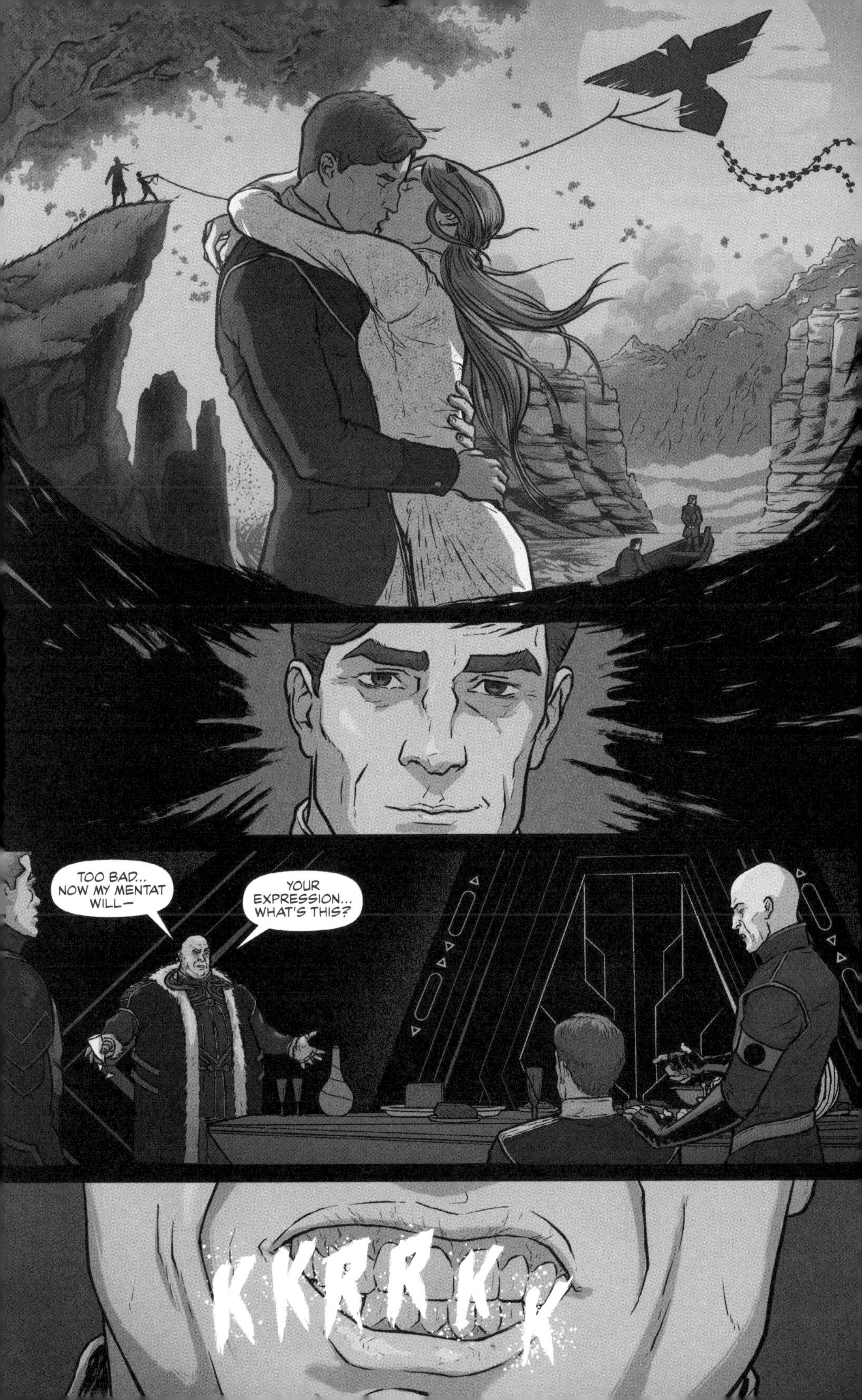
TOO BAD... NOW MY MENTAT WILL—
YOUR EXPRESSION... WHAT'S THIS?
KKRRKK

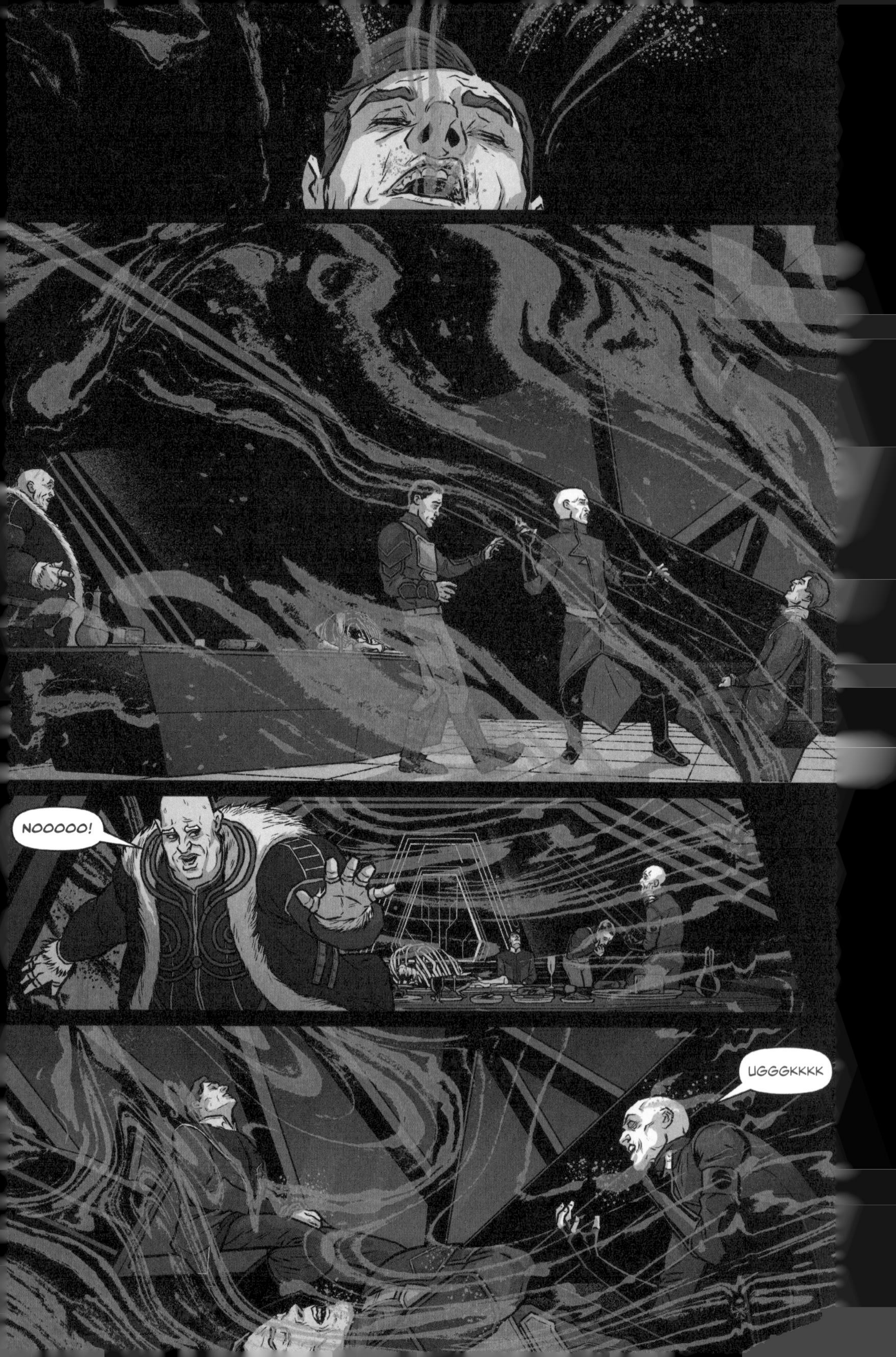
NOOOOO!
UGGGKKKK

WHAMMMM

DID I BREATHE IT? DID IT GET ME, TOO?

I'M STILL STANDING. I'M STILL BREATHING. MERCILESS HELL! THAT WAS CLOSE!

PITER GOT HIMSELF KILLED. THE FOOL! AND THAT GUARD CAPTAIN SWORE HE HAD SCOPED ALL THE CAPTIVES.

HOW DID THE DUKE MANAGE IT? IF NOT FOR THAT FLICKER IN HIS EXPRESSION...

THE NEXT GUARD CAPTAIN WILL BEGIN BY FINDING ANSWERS TO THESE QUESTIONS.

CORRIDOR CLEAR, M'LORD.

NONE OF THE STUFF ESCAPED. WE HAVE THE ROOM CLEANED OUT NOW. WHAT ARE YOUR ORDERS?

THEY'RE ALL DEAD IN THERE?

YES, M'LORD.

I WAS OUTSIDE WATCHING AND SAW THAT IT MUST BE POISON GAS. VENTILATORS IN YOUR ROOM WERE PULLING AIR IN FROM THESE CORRIDORS.

EFFICIENT, THIS ONE...WE MUST ADJUST. WHAT'S HIS NAME AGAIN? AHHH, IAKIN NEFUD.

FIRST, LET ME CONGRATULATE YOU, NEFUD. YOU'RE THE NEW CAPTAIN OF MY GUARD.

AND I HOPE YOU'LL TAKE TO HEART THE LESSON TO BE LEARNED FROM THE FATE OF YOUR PREDECESSOR.

MY LORD KNOWS I'LL DEVOTE MYSELF **ENTIRELY** TO HIS SAFETY.

YES. WELL, TO BUSINESS.

I MUST NOT SHOW HOW MUCH THIS HAS AFFECTED ME...

I SUSPECT THE DUKE HAD SOMETHING IN HIS MOUTH.

YOU WILL FIND OUT WHAT THAT SOMETHING WAS, HOW IT WAS USED, WHO HELPED HIM PUT IT THERE.

YOU'LL TAKE EVERY PRECAUTION—

NOTE THE DISDAIN, THE LACK OF RESPECT.

GET YOUR HANDS OFF ME, YOU PACK OF CARRION-EATERS!

HE'S A SARDAUKAR OFFICER, ONE OF THOSE SENT BY THE EMPEROR HIMSELF, IN DISGUISE.

SO?

TELL YOUR MEN THEY ARE NOT TO PREVENT ME FROM SEEING YOU, BARON.

I WILL NOT LOSE FACE IN FRONT OF MY MEN!

MY EMPEROR HAS CHARGED ME TO MAKE CERTAIN HIS ROYAL COUSIN DIES CLEANLY WITHOUT AGONY.

SUCH WERE THE IMPERIAL ORDERS TO ME. DID YOU THINK I'D DISOBEY?

THE DUKE'S ALREADY DEAD, IF YOU MUST KNOW.

HOW? I'M TO REPORT TO MY EMPEROR WHAT I SEE WITH MY OWN EYES. SHOW ME THE BODY.

DEAD BY HIS OWN HAND, POISON. NEFUD, SHOW HIM WHAT HE NEEDS TO SEE. I HIDE NOTHING FROM MY EMPEROR.

DAMN HIM! THIS IS TOO MUCH. NOW HE WILL SEE THAT I WAS ALMOST KILLED. HE'LL SEE THE ROOM BEFORE A THING'S BEEN CHANGED.

THERE'S NO PREVENTING IT...

I'LL HAVE TO PUT RABBAN OVER THIS DAMNABLE PLANET ONCE MORE.

WITHOUT RESTRAINT, SO THAT ARRAKIS WILL BE IN PROPER CONDITION FOR ACCEPTING FEYD-RAUTHA.

DAMN THAT PITER! HE WOULD GET HIMSELF KILLED BEFORE I WAS THROUGH WITH HIM.

AND NOW I NEED A NEW MENTAT.

146

IN THE DESERT, HIDING LIKE A CHILD...WHEN I'M NOW THE DUKE.

I'M NOW THE DUKE!

YUEH THE TRAITOR...
YUEH LEFT US THE
PACK, THE SUPPLIES.

YUEH MADE THE
PLANS. HE SET
THIS UP.

RUN,
PAUL!

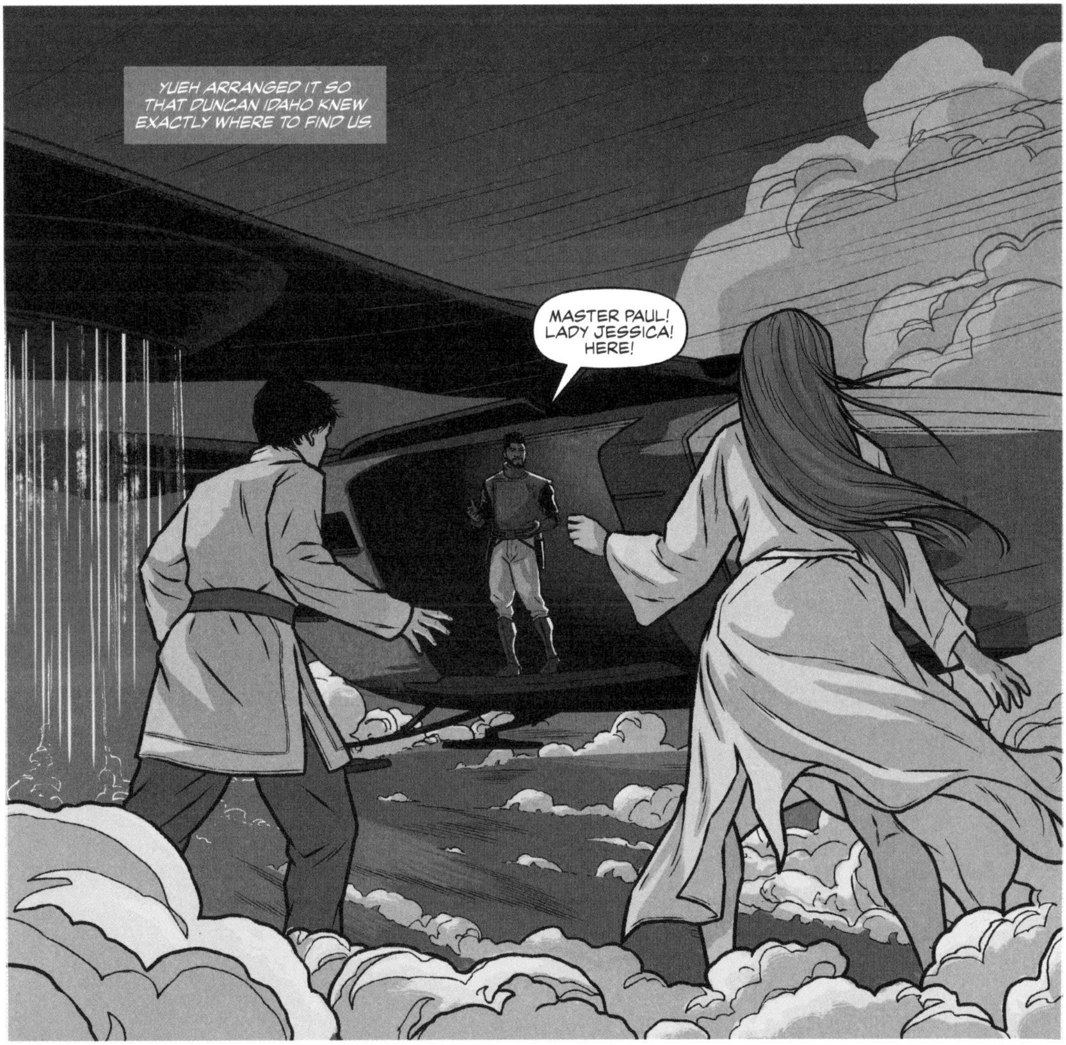
YUEH ARRANGED IT SO THAT DUNCAN IDAHO KNEW EXACTLY WHERE TO FIND US.
MASTER PAUL! LADY JESSICA! HERE!

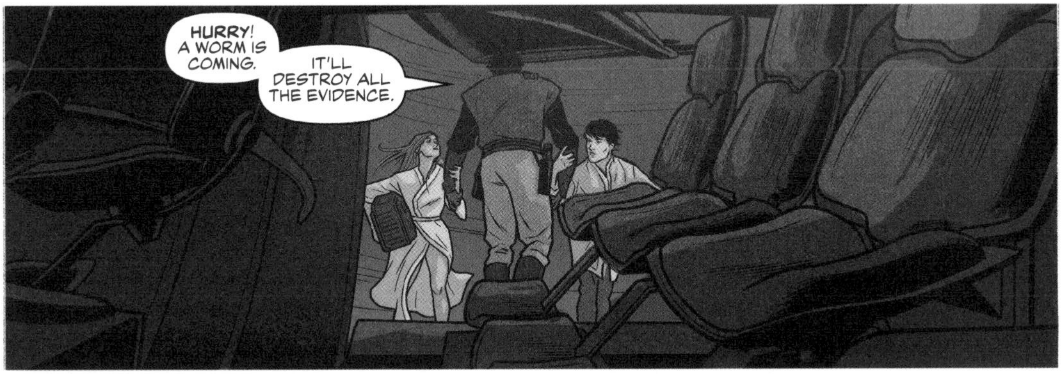
HURRY! A WORM IS COMING.
IT'LL DESTROY ALL THE EVIDENCE.

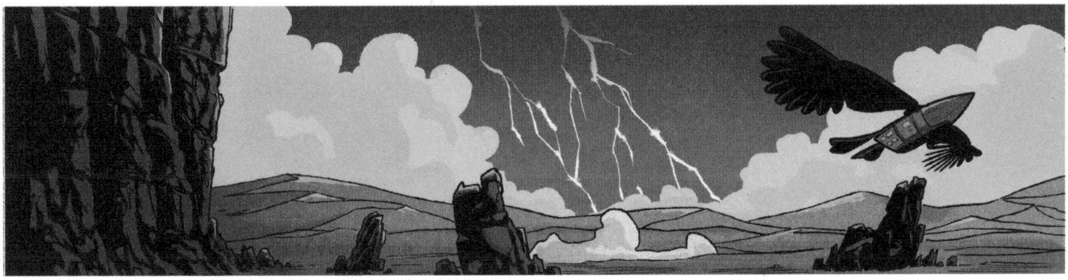

ARRAKEEN HAS FALLEN, THE RESIDENCY OVERRUN. HARKONNEN ANIMALS EVERYWHERE.

YUEH TOLD ME WHERE TO FIND YOU, TOLD ME I HAD NO CHOICE.

YOU DID WHAT YOU HAD TO DO, DUNCAN.

I'VE BEEN LISTENING TO RADIO CHATTER, ALL CHANNELS. IT'S NOT JUST HARKONNENS.

I HEARD SARDAUKAR BATTLE LANGUAGE. THE EMPEROR HIMSELF SENT HIS CRACK TROOPS.

THE ATREIDES HAVE BEEN BETRAYED... DESTROYED. BUT WE HAVE TO SURVIVE. OUT IN THE DESERT?

THE PACK YUEH LEFT FOR US HAS STILLSUITS, WATER, A STILLTENT.

WAIT HERE FOR ME, AND HIDE.

I HAVE TO MAKE CERTAIN... **ARRANGEMENTS** WITH THE PLANETOLOGIST KYNES. I'LL BE BACK FOR YOU. THE FREMKIT HAS EVERYTHING YOU NEED.

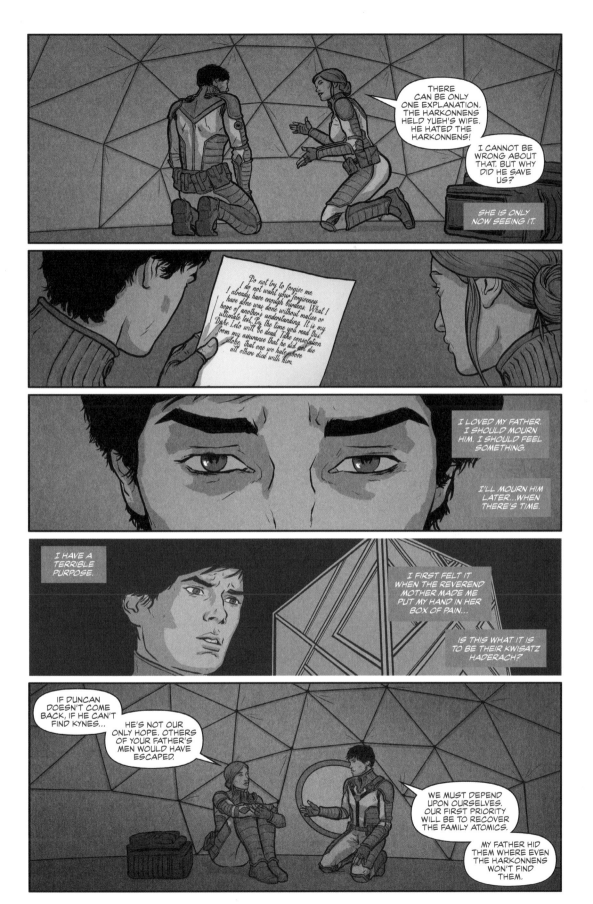

THERE CAN BE ONLY ONE EXPLANATION. THE HARKONNENS HELD YUEH'S WIFE. HE HATED THE HARKONNENS!

I CANNOT BE WRONG ABOUT THAT. BUT WHY DID HE SAVE US?

SHE IS ONLY NOW SEEING IT.

Do not try to forgive me. I do not want your forgiveness. I already have enough burdens. What I have done was done without malice or hope of another's understanding. It is my ultimate test. By the time you read this, Duke Leto will be dead. Take consolation from my assurance that he did not die alone, that one we hate above all others died with him.

I LOVED MY FATHER. I SHOULD MOURN HIM. I SHOULD FEEL SOMETHING.

I'LL MOURN HIM LATER...WHEN THERE'S TIME.

I HAVE A TERRIBLE PURPOSE.

I FIRST FELT IT WHEN THE REVEREND MOTHER MADE ME PUT MY HAND IN HER BOX OF PAIN...

IS THIS WHAT IT IS TO BE THEIR KWISATZ HADERACH?

IF DUNCAN DOESN'T COME BACK, IF HE CAN'T FIND KYNES...

HE'S NOT OUR ONLY HOPE. OTHERS OF YOUR FATHER'S MEN WOULD HAVE ESCAPED.

WE MUST DEPEND UPON OURSELVES. OUR FIRST PRIORITY WILL BE TO RECOVER THE FAMILY ATOMICS.

MY FATHER HID THEM WHERE EVEN THE HARKONNENS WON'T FIND THEM.

THIS IS THE WAY IT HAD TO BE, LETO. A TIME OF LOVE AND A TIME OF GRIEF.

I HAVE THE ATREIDES DAUGHTER I WAS ORDERED TO PRODUCE, BUT THE REVEREND MOTHER WAS WRONG.

A DAUGHTER WOULDN'T HAVE SAVED MY LETO. I CONCEIVED OUT OF INSTINCT AND NOT OUT OF OBEDIENCE.

WE HAVE TWO LITERJONS OF WATER. IT'LL BE DAWN SOON. WE CAN WAIT THROUGH THE DAY FOR IDAHO, BUT NOT THROUGH ANOTHER NIGHT.

IN THE DESERT, YOU MUST TRAVEL BY NIGHT AND REST IN SHADE THROUGH THE DAY.

IF WE LEAVE HERE, IDAHO CAN'T FIND US.

AND EVEN THESE STILLSUITS WILL ONLY KEEP US ALIVE SO LONG.

LITERJONS, STILLTENT, ENERGY CAPS, RECATHS, SANDSNORK, BINOCULARS, STILLSUIT REPKIT, BARADYE PISTOL, SINKCHART, FILT-PLUGS, PARACOMPASS, MAKER HOOKS, THUMPERS, FREMKIT, FIRE PILLAR...

152

WHERE CAN WE POSSIBLY GO?

MY FATHER SPOKE OF DESERT POWER. THINK OF WHAT THAT MEANS.

THE HARKONNENS CAN'T RULE THIS PLANET WITHOUT IT. THINK OF THIS TENT, THESE SUPPLIES, THE PACK...WHAT IT MEANS.

SOMEONE IS PAYING THE SPACING GUILD NOT TO INSTALL WEATHER SATELLITES, BECAUSE SATELLITES SEE WHAT IS HAPPENING IN THE DEEP DESERT.

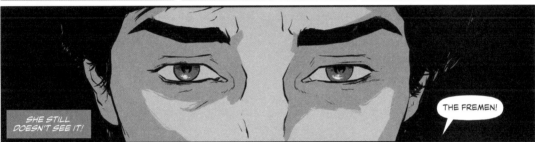

SHE STILL DOESN'T SEE IT!

THE FREMEN!

THIS IS MORE THAN A SECOND-APPROXIMATION ANSWER; IT'S THE STRAIGHT-LINE MENTAT COMPUTATION. DEPEND ON IT.

PAUL, YOU ARE NOT A MENTAT. NOT YET.

I'LL NEVER BE A MENTAT. I'M *SOMETHING ELSE*, A FREAK! LEAVE ME ALONE.

WHY CAN'T I MOURN? MY FATHER IS DEAD.

I HAVE NEVER SEEN PAUL SO DISTRESSED!

Desert Jumping Mouse, also known as muad'dib. Extremely resilient animal. Able to survive the most adverse conditions.

I'M HIS MOTHER I SHOULD COMFORT HIM.

BUT, I CAN'T...

NOW IS THE TIME TO CARRY OUT MY FATHER'S WISH. I MUST GIVE HER HIS MESSAGE NOW WHILE SHE HAS TIME FOR GRIEF.

GRIEF WOULD INCONVENIENCE US LATER.

SUCH HARSH, TERRIBLE LOGIC...

MOTHER...

MY FATHER IS DEAD.

MY FATHER CHARGED ME ONCE TO GIVE YOU A MESSAGE IF ANYTHING HAPPENED TO HIM. HE WANTED YOU TO KNOW HE **NEVER** SUSPECTED YOU.

AND HE HAD BUT ONE REGRET— THAT HE NEVER MADE YOU HIS DUCHESS.

USELESS WASTE OF WATER...

LETO, MY LETO...

I HAVE NO GRIEF. WHY? WHY?

MY VISION IS SHARPER THAN EVER, BUT IN A DIFFERENT WAY, I SEE NOT JUST ONE FUTURE, BUT MANY POSSIBILITIES.

THE HEAT AND COLD OF UNCOUNTED POSSIBILITIES...

NOT JUST ONE FUTURE, BUT **MANY** FUTURES.

ALL OF THEM REAL...

MUAD'DIB! MUAD'DIB!

MUAD'DIB! MUAD'DIB!

MUAD'DIB! MUAD'DIB!

156

MY AWARENESS HAS REACHED A POINT I NEVER IMAGINED. POSSIBILITIES, UNCOUNTED POSSIBILITIES...

PEOPLE. PLANETS. MY LIFE...MY OWN DEATH IN A THOUSAND WAYS...

I HAVE ANOTHER KIND OF SIGHT. I SEE ANOTHER KIND OF TERRAIN: THE AVAILABLE PATHS.

MAYBE THE SPACING GUILD WILL HAVE ME. WE CAN GO THERE FOR REFUGE. MY STRANGENESS WOULD BE ACCEPTED AS A THING OF HIGH VALUE.

ALL THOSE THOUGHTS, THOSE REVELATIONS, THOSE POSSIBILITIES... NO MORE THAN A HEARTBEAT HAS PASSED!

I AM A MONSTER! A FREAK!

MY MIND IS FILLED WITH DATA, ANALYSES, PROJECTIONS.

BUT THE HOLLOW INSIDE HAS NO EMOTIONS.

MY FATHER IS DEAD. WHERE IS MY GRIEF?

157

NO! NO, NO, NO!

I'M HERE, PAUL. IT'S ALL RIGHT. WHAT'S WRONG?

YOU!

WHAT HAVE YOU DONE TO ME?

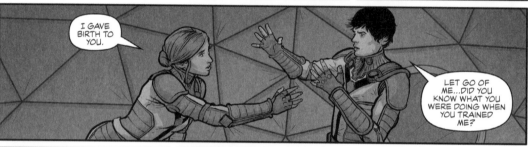

I GAVE BIRTH TO YOU.

LET GO OF ME...DID YOU KNOW WHAT YOU WERE DOING WHEN YOU TRAINED ME?

I HOPED THE THING ANY PARENT HOPES—THAT YOU'D BE...SUPERIOR, DIFFERENT.

DIFFERENT?

YOU DIDN'T WANT A SON—YOU WANTED A KWISATZ HADERACH!

YOUR TRAINING, MY HEREDITY, THIS PLACE...ALL THOSE THINGS HAVE AWAKENED **THE SLEEPER.** IT'S HERE, IN ME. IT GOES ON AND ON AND ON AND ON AND—

DO YOU KNOW WHY?

THE SPICE! IT'S IN EVERYTHING HERE—THE AIR, THE SOIL, THE FOOD. **THE GERIATRIC** SPICE. IT'S LIKE THE TRUTHSAYER DRUG. IT'S A POISON!

THE SPICE CHANGES ANYONE WHO GETS THIS MUCH OF IT, BUT THANKS TO YOU, I COULD BRING THE CHANGE TO CONSCIOUSNESS. I CAN SEE IT.

WE'RE TRAPPED HERE. THE SPICE IS ADDICTIVE. IT WILL KEEP US HERE ON ARRAKIS.

I MUST TELL YOU ABOUT MY WAKING DREAM, MOTHER.

TO BE SURE YOU ACCEPT WHAT I SAY, I'LL TELL YOU FIRST THAT I KNOW YOU'LL BEAR A DAUGHTER, MY SISTER, HERE ON ARRAKIS.

NO ONE KNOWS THAT! NOT EVEN LETO!

WE EXIST ONLY TO SERVE.

WE'LL FIND A HOME AMONG THE FREMEN.

YOUR SISTERHOOD'S MISSIONARIA PROTECTIVA HAS BOUGHT US A BOLT HOLE.

HOW DOES HE KNOW ABOUT THE MISSIONARIA PROTECTIVA? ONLY THE BENE GESSERIT KNOW...

"THIS SENSE OF THE FUTURE—I SEEM TO HAVE NO CONTROL AOVER IT.

SOME PLACES I DON'T SEE...SHADOWED PLACES...AS THOUGH IT WENT BEHIND A HILL. AND THERE ARE BRANCHINGS..."

I RECOGNIZE MY OWN TERRIBLE PURPOSE—THE PRESSURE OF MY LIFE SPREADING OUTWARD LIKE AN EXPANDING BUBBLE...

TIME RETREATING BEFORE IT.

HE HAS THE LOOK OF TERRIBLE AWARENESS, OF SOMEONE FORCED TO THE KNOWLEDGE OF HIS OWN MORTALITY. HE IS NO LONGER A CHILD.

I'M ACTIVATING THE GLOWTAB, PAUL.

LIGHT...IT DRIVES BACK THE SHADOWS.

PAUL, WE HAVE TO THINK OF OUR SURVIVAL NOW.

THERE'S A WAY TO EVADE THE HARKONNENS.

THE HARKONNENS! PUT THOSE TWISTED HUMANS OUT OF YOUR MIND.

I SEE SO MUCH NOW. THINK, MOTHER.

YOU SHOULD KNOW THIS—WE ARE HARKONNENS!

WHEN NEXT YOU FIND A MIRROR, STUDY YOUR FACE—STUDY MINE NOW.

THE TRACES ARE THERE IF YOU DON'T BLIND YOURSELF.

TAKE MY WORD FOR IT. I'VE WALKED THE FUTURE, I HAVE ALL THE DATA. WE'RE HARKONNENS.

A...RENEGADE BRANCH OF THE FAMILY?

YOU'RE THE BARON'S OWN **DAUGHTER**.

THE BARON SAMPLED MANY PLEASURES IN HIS YOUTH, AND ONCE PERMITTED HIMSELF TO BE SEDUCED.

BUT IT WAS FOR THE GENETIC PURPOSES OF THE BENE GESSERIT, DONE BY ONE OF YOU!

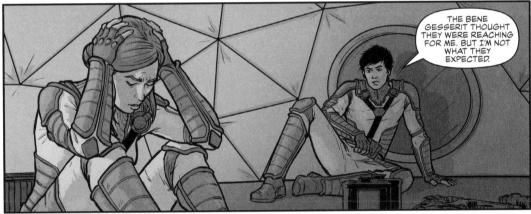

THE BENE GESSERIT THOUGHT THEY WERE REACHING FOR ME. BUT I'M NOT WHAT THEY EXPECTED.

GREAT MOTHER! HE'S THE KWISATZ HADERACH!

YOU'RE THINKING I'M THE KWISATZ HADERACH. PUT THAT OUT OF YOUR MIND. I'M SOMETHING UNEXPECTED.

I'VE ARRIVED BEFORE MY TIME. AND THEY DON'T KNOW IT.

THE BENE GESSERIT WON'T LEARN ABOUT ME UNTIL IT'S TOO LATE...

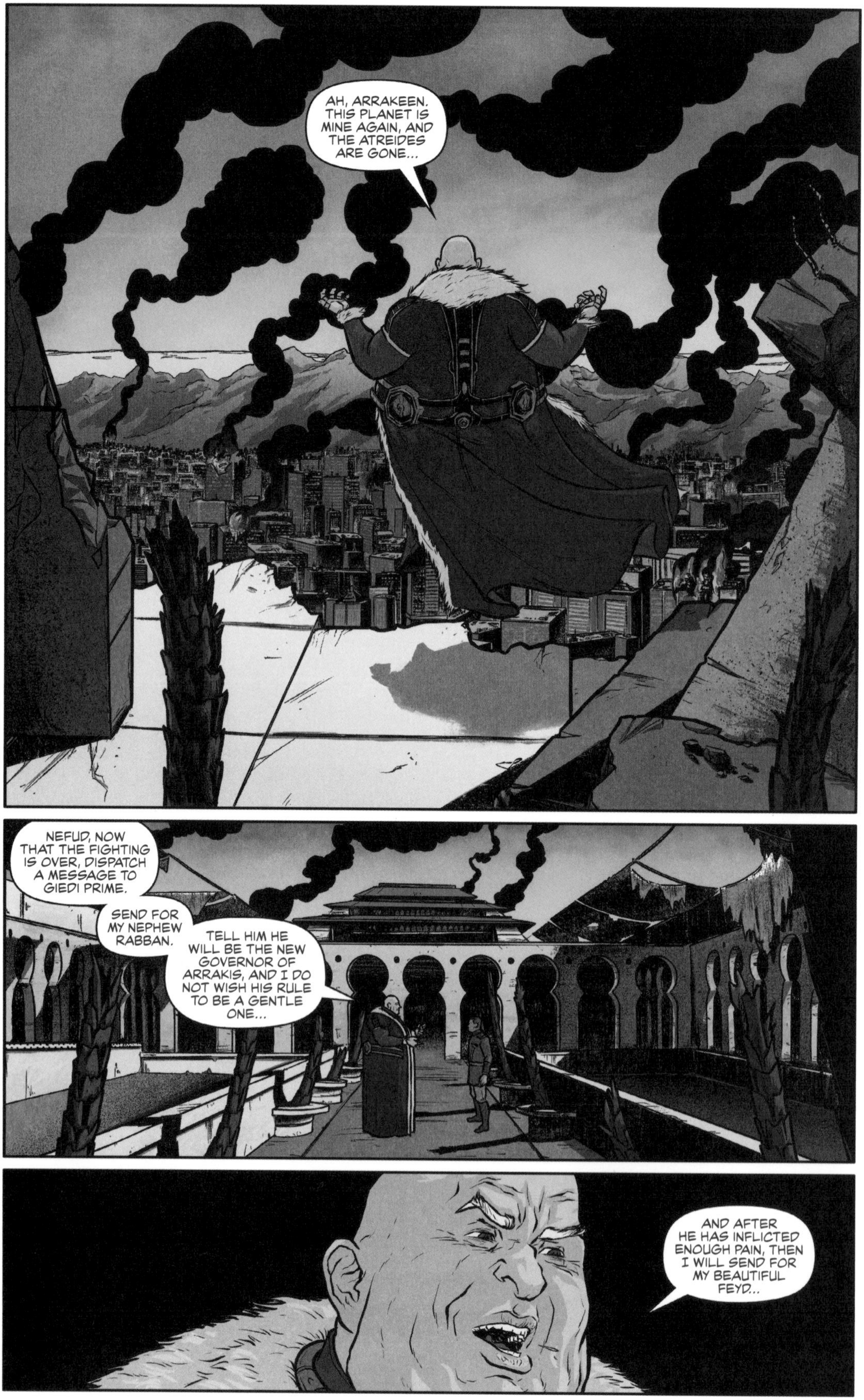
AH, ARRAKEEN. THIS PLANET IS MINE AGAIN, AND THE ATREIDES ARE GONE...
NEFUD, NOW THAT THE FIGHTING IS OVER, DISPATCH A MESSAGE TO GIEDI PRIME.
SEND FOR MY NEPHEW RABBAN.
TELL HIM HE WILL BE THE NEW GOVERNOR OF ARRAKIS, AND I DO NOT WISH HIS RULE TO BE A GENTLE ONE...
AND AFTER HE HAS INFLICTED ENOUGH PAIN, THEN I WILL SEND FOR MY BEAUTIFUL FEYD...

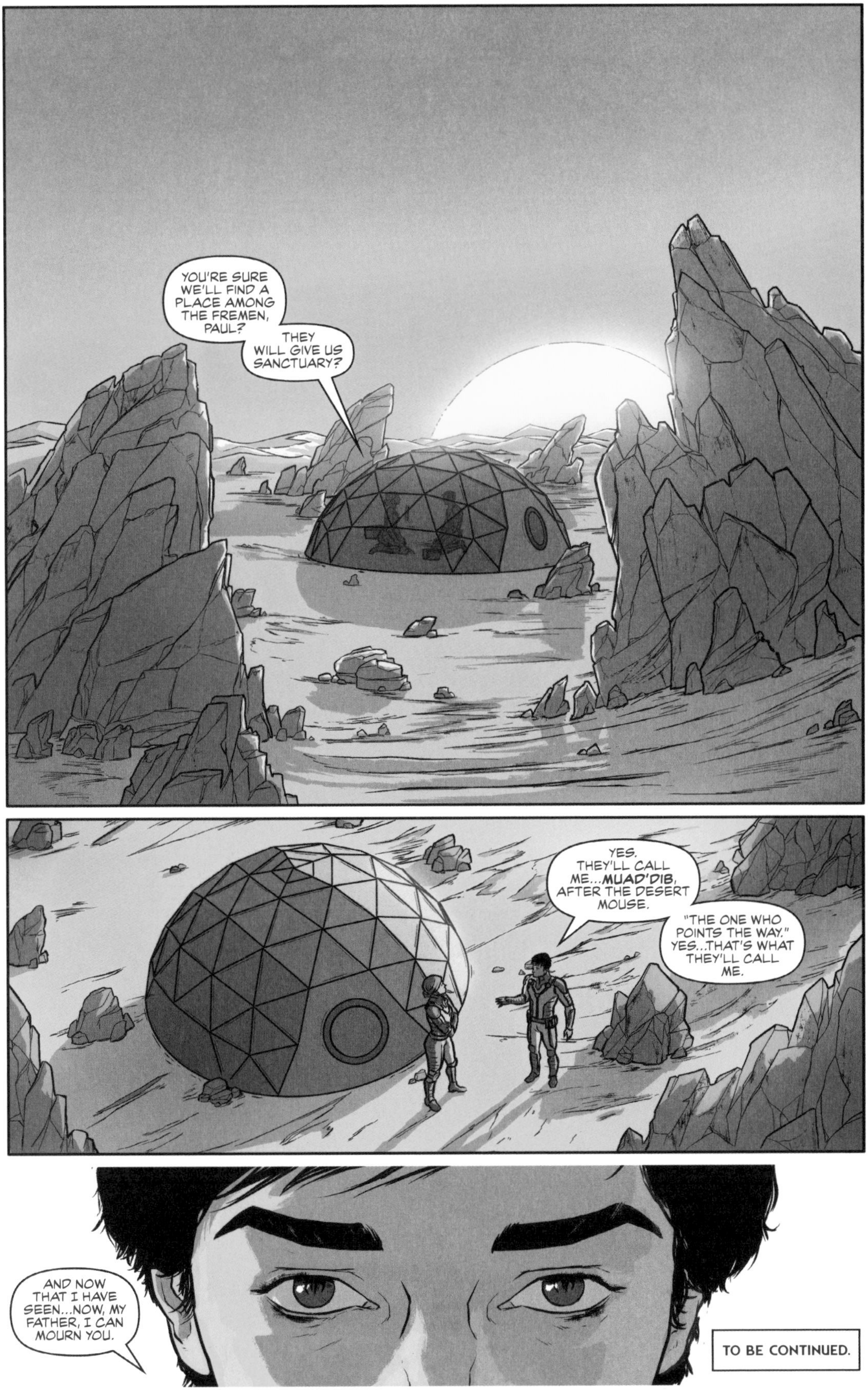
YOU'RE SURE WE'LL FIND A PLACE AMONG THE FREMEN, PAUL?
THEY WILL GIVE US SANCTUARY?
YES. THEY'LL CALL ME...**MUAD'DIB**, AFTER THE DESERT MOUSE.
"THE ONE WHO POINTS THE WAY." YES...THAT'S WHAT THEY'LL CALL ME.
AND NOW THAT I HAVE SEEN...NOW, MY FATHER, I CAN MOURN YOU.
TO BE CONTINUED.

DUNE

THE GRAPHIC NOVEL, BOOK 2

MUAD'DIB

COMING SPRING 2022

FRANK HERBERT (1920–86) was an American science-fiction writer best known for his novel *Dune* and its subsequent five sequels. Though Herbert did not graduate from university, he became famous for his science-fiction works, and *Dune* is arguably the most admired science-fiction novel of all time. The series is widely considered the archetype for all science fiction that followed.

BRIAN HERBERT, the son of Frank Herbert, has written a moving biography of his father, *Dreamer of Dune*. Brian is also known for his collaborations with author Kevin J. Anderson, with whom he has written multiple sequels and prequels to his father's landmark 1965 science-fiction novel *Dune*, all of which have made the *New York Times* bestseller list.

KEVIN J. ANDERSON is an American science-fiction author of more than fifty bestsellers. He has written spin-off novels for Star Wars, StarCraft, and The X-Files and, with Brian Herbert, is the co-author of the *Dune* prequel series. He currently resides near Monument, Colorado, with his wife.

RAÚL ALLÉN is an artist and director living in Valladolíd, Spain. Allén has worked for Marvel Comics, Valiant, and DC Comics with writers such as Matt Fraction, Jeff Lemire, Matt Kindt, and Peter Milligan. As an illustrator, Allén has worked with Quentin Tarantino, *Playboy*, *Rolling Stone*, the *New York Times*, and the *Wall Street Journal*.

PATRICIA MARTÍN is a letterer, comics artist, and illustrator, nominated for multiple Harvey Awards. For the last four years she has worked on *Wonder Woman* with Steve Orlando, *Bloodshot Reborn* with Jeff Lemire, *Ninjak* with Matt Kindt, and *Secret Weapons* alongside artist Raúl Allén and writer Eric Heisserer. She lives in Spain.

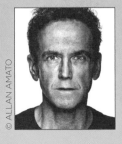

BILL SIENKIEWICZ is an Eisner-winning, Emmy-nominated artist best known for revamping the style of comic and graphic novel illustration from 1980 onward, most notably with Marvel Comics and DC Comics. In 1984, Sienkiewicz was chosen by David Lynch to illustrate the comic book adaptation of his *Dune* movie.